蔡志忠 /编绘

[美] 布莱恩·布雅 /译

尊者的棒喝 曹溪的佛唱

禅说·六祖坛经

ZEN STORIES · WISDOM OF THE ZEN MASTERS

The Staff and Shout of the Venerable Ones
The Quest For Enlightenment

中国出版集团

现代出版社

图字：01-2005-2344

图书在版编目（ＣＩＰ）数据

禅说·六祖坛经 / 蔡志忠编绘；（美）布雅
（Bruya, B.）译. -- 北京：现代出版社, 2013.10
（蔡志忠漫画中国传统文化经典：中英文对照版）
ISBN 978-7-5143-1870-8

Ⅰ. ①禅… Ⅱ. ①蔡… ②布… Ⅲ. ①漫画—连环画
—作品集—中国—现代 Ⅳ. ① J228.2

中国版本图书馆 CIP 数据核字（2013）第 240304 号

蔡志忠漫画中国传统文化经典：中英文对照版

禅说·六祖坛经

作　　者	蔡志忠　编绘	
	［美］布莱恩·布雅（BRIAN BRUYA）译	
责任编辑	袁　涛	
出版发行	现代出版社	
地　　址	北京市安定门外安华里 504 号	
邮政编码	100011	
电　　话	010-64267325　010-64245264（兼传真）	
网　　址	www.1980xd.com	
电子信箱	xiandai@cnpitc.com.cn	
印　　刷	北京诚信伟业印刷有限公司	
开　　本	710×1000　1 / 16	
印　　张	18	
版　　次	2013 年 11 月第 1 版　2014 年 4 月第 2 次印刷	
书　　号	ISBN 978-7-5143-1870-8	
定　　价	35.00 元	

目录
contents

不立文字
教外别传
直指人心
见性成佛
Not reliant on the written word,
A Special transmission separate from the
scriptures;
Direct potinting at one's mind,
Seeing one's nature, becoming the Buddha.

何谓"禅"？
What is Zen?

一条小鱼向大鱼问道：
A baby fish once asked an elder fish:

我常听人说起海的事情，可是海是什么？
I keep hearing people talk about this thing called the sea. Just what is the sea?

你的周围就是海啊！
The sea is what surrounds you.

可是我怎么看不到？
But why can't I see it?

海在你里面、也在你外面，你生于海终归于海。海包围着你，就像你自己的身体。
The sea is within you and all around you. You were born in the sea and will die in the sea. The sea enveliopes you, just like your own skin does.

庄子说：鱼相忘乎江湖，人相忘乎道术。人活在禅海之中，但却不知道禅是何物？想知道什么是禅吗？请继续看下去……
Confucius said, "Fish forget that they live in lakes and rivers; people forget that they live in the magie of the Dao(Tao)." People live in s sea of Zen (chan/ch'an), yet they don't kno what it is. Would you like to know what Zen is? Please, read on...

波浪的觉悟
Enlightenment of the Wave

杯茶禅理
A Cup of Zen

1

一位学者向"南隐"问禅，南隐以茶相待。
One day, a scholar went to see a Zen monk named Nanin to inquire about Zen. Nanin treated his guest to a cup of tea.

2

他将茶水倒入杯中，茶满了但他还是继续倒……
He poured the tea into a cup, and when the cup was full, he kept right on pouring....

3

师父，茶已经漫出来了，不要再倒了。
Master, that's enough! It's full!

4

你就像这只茶杯一样，里面装满了你自己的看法、想法。你不先把你自己的杯子清空，叫我如何对你说禅？
You are just like this cup — Full of your own thoughts and ideas. If you don't first empty yourself, how can I teach you about Zen?

是
Oui.

心中有自己的成见，就听不见别人的真言。两人对谈，多数人急着表达自己的意见，结果除了听到自己的声音以外，什么都不曾得到。
If your mind is filled with your own prejudices, the truth that others speak can't be heard. When engaging in conversation, most people are in a hurry to express their own opinion, and as a result, they don't hear anythingbut the sound of their own voice.

4

悟道的结果
The outcome of Enlighten- ment

1
自古以来，很多人离开了他的家园亲人，遁入佛门去参禅。
Ever since ancient times, many people have left their homes and loved ones to enter the gates of Buddhism and study Zen meditation.

2
他们不惜费那么大的功夫去钻研参究，究竟能得到什么呢？
They expend a great amount of time and energy in disciplined contemplative training, but what is it that they gain?

3
以这个问题去问了悟的禅师们，通常他们会回答说：
If this question were posed to enlightened Zen masters, they would most likely answer :

4

無

Nothing

当人停止分别、妄想和思维活动时，理、事二障当下消除，内心充满安详，自然就"无"处不通。
When we stop differentiating, halt our delusions, and put an end to all thoughts, the two hindrances of discursive thought and intention will dissolve, and as our minds fill with peace, naturally,there will be "nothing" we won't understand.

欲断绝烦恼妄想的根源而修行，不只是为了达至真空无想、无念、无心、无我的静寂中等境界，而是要求得日常不一样的生活行为中所体验到而滋生出来的妙智慧。在那种境界中，全世界都在一望之中而没有对立，此即是超越了自己、他人和善恶之真实世界。"迷时三界有，悟后十方空"，但是，如何悟得"无"和"空"的境界呢？

If one engages in self-cultivation with the desire to sever the roots of defilement and erroneous thinking, it is not only to attain the tranquil realm of true emptiness which involves no-thought, no-idea, no-mind, no-self, etc.; it is also in pursuit of the wonderful wisdom that is experienced in and grows from a way of life that is different from the ordinary. In that realm, the whole world is seen from one perspective, and there are no dichotomies; it is the true world where the self and others, as well as good and evil, are all transcended. "In confusion, the three realms exist; after enlightenment, the ten directions are empty." But how do we attain the realm of Nothingness and Emptiness?

禅　说
尊者的棒喝
The Staff and Shout of the Venerable Ones
Zen Stories

以心传心
Passing
on
the Mind

1　佛祖释尊在灵鹫山，登上高座准备说话。
One day on Vulture Peak, the founder of Buddhism, Siddhartha Gautama(Sakyamuni the Buddha), was preparing to speak.

2　忽然释尊拿出一朵花，眼观众弟子的反应，众人都不明白佛祖的意思，而默默不语。
Suddenly, he pilled out a flower, watching for the reaction of his disciples. Not understanding the Buddha's intent, they just sat there silently.

只有摩诃迦叶尊者破颜微笑。
Only the venerable Kasyapa boke into a smile.

3　4

我悟道的方法是看透一切，包容一切，以喜悦的心去看清事物的本来面目。
My method of enlightenment is to see through everything, to embrace everything, and to approach things with a happy heart, seeing clearly their original face.

这种微妙的法门是超越文字，超越数学理论的。
This mysterious dharma transcends both language and rational principles.

6

不能用逻辑思考，而是要用体会才能了解领悟的。
Logical thinking cannot be used to attain enlightenment, Instead, one must use intuition.

5

7

刚才摩诃迦叶尊者已经领悟而起共鸣，所以我要将禅心传给他。
Just now, the venerable Kasyapa revealed his understanding. Therefore, I shall pass on to him the Zen mind.

8

禅即是——不污染的宇宙真理和不污染的生命之心产生共鸣而有所领悟，并持续不污染之心安然自得。
Zen is: enlightenment proceeding from the resonance between the principles of an unpolluted universe and the mind of an unpolluted life, allowing the unpolluted mind to continue on in peaceful contentedness.

把握现时
Seize
the
Moment

1
世尊问弟子说:
Sakyamuni asked his disciples:

人生究竟有多长?
How long is a person's life?

2
五十年。
Fifty.

3
不对。
Wrong.

四十年。
Forty?

不对,
不对!
No.

三十年。
Thirty.

4

5
不对。
Wrong.

那么人生究竟有多长?
How long is a person's life?

6

7
人生只在呼吸间。
Life is but abresth.

不要沉湎于昨日、明日的世界中,而应生活在"今日"的世界里,应随时随地体会到"当下"周边美好的事物。
Don't get mired in the Worlds of yesterday and tomorrow. Instead, live in the world of today. Wherever you are and whatever you are doing, experience the beautiful things around you at that moment.

迦叶刹竿
Kasyapa
and the
Flagpole

1
世尊在灵山法会上将衣钵传给迦叶。
During the Buddhist gathering on Vnlture Peak, Sakyamuni Passed his robe and alms bowl on to Kasyapa

阿难问迦叶尊者说：
Ananda asked the venerable Kasyapa

世尊传金襕袈裟外，还传了什么？
Besides the brocaded robe, what else did Sakyamuni give you?

阿难！
Ananda!
3

是！
Yes!
4

2

天晚了，去把寺前刹竿收起来。
It's late. Go take down the flagpole out front.

！

5

平常心即是道，不要往虚无缥缈的世界去找佛理，只要注意生活上的细节，在生活上去体认即可。
The ordinary mind is the Dao. You needn't track through an illusory world to find the principles of buddhism. Just pay attention to the details of life and try to understand things intuitively, that's all.

渡女过河
Carrying a Woman across a Rive

1

坦山和尚与一年轻和尚走在路上看见一位漂亮的女孩过不了河。
One day while the Zen monk Tanzan and a young monk were traveling, they happened upon a beautiful young lady in distress.

2

我抱你过河。
Here, let me carry you across.

3

师父，谢谢您，再见！
Thank you very much.Good-bye!

4

他俩继续走了半天路程……
The two continued on their Journey for more than half a day...

5

我们出家人不是不近女色吗？刚才你为什么要那样做？
I thought we monks were supposed to avoid women. Why did you just do that?

哦！你说那个女人吗？
Huh? Oh, you mean that woman way back there?

我早就把她放下了，你还抱着吗？
I Put her down long ago. Are you still carrying her?

6

渡人过河的，心中并没有抱持着女色，坦然无牵无挂。一直抱持着女色的不正是那个小和尚吗？
Tanzan carried a person across s river, but in his mind he wasn't carrying a woman; he was completely detached and had no misgivings. The one who was really carrying a woman seems to have been the younger monk, wouldn't you say?

呆头大官
The Lamebrain Official

1

大愚和愚堂两位禅师奉邀去见一位想学禅的大官。
The Zen masters Dayu and Yutang accepted an invitation to instruct a major official interested in Zen.

你天性聪敏，能够学禅。
You are a naturally intelligent and receptive man. in think you will make a rine student of Zen.

2

胡说！这呆头虽居高位，但对禅一窍不通！
You've got to be kidding! This lamebrain may have a high position, but he wouldn't know Zen if he were hit over the head with it!

3

听了两位高见，我知道该怎么做了。
After listening to your two honorable opinions, I have decided what to do.

4

结果这位大官没有为愚堂建庙，却给大愚造了一座，且跟他学禅。
In the end, not only did the official not buidl a temple for Yutang, he built one for Dayu instead and studied Zen with him.

大愚不因为对象是大官，而直指出真实，结果受重用。不受外相迷惑，心中没有善恶二元的境地，才是接近了禅。
Disregarding the high position of the official,Dayu spoke exactly what was on his mind, and as a result, was held in high regard for it. Don't be deluded by exterior circumstances. When the dualism of good and evil is gone from your mind, only then will you be nearing Zen.

墨竹朱竹
Black Bamboo,
Red Bamboo

1　有人请一位画家画一幅竹。
There was once an aritist who was asked to do a painting of bamboo.

3　可是颜色错了，你将竹子画成红色了……
But there seems to be a problem with the color. You painted the bamboo red...

太好了！
太棒了！
Fantastic!
Marvelous!

你想画什么颜色的呢？
And what color would you have it be?

当然是黑色的。
Black, of course.

4　有谁见过黑色的竹子呢？
Who's ever seen black bamboo?

当你指责着别人的错误时，很可能你自己所抱持的观念也是错误的，还自以为对呢！
When you go pointing out other people's mistakes, the real error may very well be hidden in your own misconceptions!

5

16

生死有序
The Order of Life and Death

1 一位富人向仙崖和尚求墨宝……
There was once a wealthy man who asked the Zen monk Sengai to create a work of calligraphy for him...

2 父死 子死 孙死
Father Dies Son Dies Grandson Dies

仙崖和尚
Sengai

哇！
Ahhhh!

我是请你写吉祥好词，你怎么开这种玩笑？
I wanted you to write something auspicious! What are you trying to pull?

3 这是好词啊！
This is auspicious.

4 假如你的儿子先你而死，你将十分悲痛，假如你的孙子在你儿子之前死了，你父子将十分悲痛。
If your sons were to die before you, or if your grandsons were to die before your sons, you would be extremely unhappy.

5 如果你家人一代一代地照我写的次序死，那叫做享尽天年，这才是真正的兴旺啊！
If the people in your family live generation after generation and die according to this order, what is more auspicious than that?

有道理！
That makes sense.

生为徭役，死为休息。"死"像一个游子回到家一样。人人能享尽天年，按次序死不正是更大的福气吗？
"Life is taxing, death is relaxing" (Zhuangzi). Death is like a weary traveler returning home. Isn't it the most fortunate thing for everyone to die in their natural order?

不语戒
Vow of Silence

四个学僧互相约定：静默打坐七天中不得开口说话……
Four monks made a pact: they would meditate in silence for seven days, during which time, no ome was to say a single word...

1

头一天他们都静默不语，但到了深夜，烛火忽明忽暗……
Late at night on the first day, their one candle suddenly started to flicker...

2

啊，火要熄了！
Oh no, the candle's about to go out!

3

我们应该一言不发的呀！
Remember, now, we're not supposed to talk.

4

你们为什么要讲话呢？
Why do you guys keep talking?

5

哈哈哈哈，只有我没有讲话！
Ha, ha! I'm the only one who didn't say anything!

6

很多人在告诫别人，指正别人的错误时，很可能自己也正抱持着"错误"。
When pointing out other people's faults, we often forget that we may be guilty of the same mistake.

一切皆空
Everything is Empty

1 铁舟到处参访名师，一天，他来到相国寺见独园和尚……
Therr was once a monk named tesshu who traveled the land meeting with all the best Zen masters. One day, he wandered into Shokoku Temple and happened upon the monk Dokuou...

表述他的悟境，他十分得意。
Here, he proudly proclaimed his leved of enlightenment.

心、佛，以及众生，三者皆是空……
The mind, the Buddha, and all beings are empty...

2 3

现象的真性是空。无悟、无迷、无圣、无凡、无施、无受。
The true nature of all things is emptiness. No enlightenment, no delusion; no sages, no commoners; no toil, no reward.

4 当！
Ow!

哎呀！
Bonk!

6 "无善无恶，不受苦乐，一切皆空。"连这一句都不足与外人道，铁舟拥有的不过是口头禅罢了。
"There is no good or evil, no suffering or pleasure; everything is empty."Even this sentence isn't worth saying to anyone. Tesshu had only a superficial understanding of Zen.

一切皆空，哪儿来这么大的脾气？
If everything is empty, where did that temper come from?

5 您干吗打我？
What did you do that for?!

佛在家中
The buddha is in the Home

杨黼离别双亲到四川去拜访无际菩萨……
One day, a young man named Yang Fu left his parents to go Sichuan (Szechwan) to vist the bodhisattva, Wuji.

1

你去哪里？
Where are you going, young mans?

我去拜无际菩萨为师……
I am going to study under Wuji, the bodhisattva.

tea 茶

2

与其去找菩萨，还不如去找佛。
Instead of looking for a mere bodhisatttva, you'd be better off looking for the Buddha.

哪里有佛？
Do you know where I can find the Buddha?

3

你回家时，看到有个人披着毯子，反穿鞋来迎接你，那就是佛。
Where you return home, a person wearing a blanket and with shoes on the wrong feet will come to greet you. That person is the Buddha.

是！
Right!

4

他依照吩咐，回到家里已是深夜了……
Yang Fu hurried back, arriving at his home late at night...

5

他的母亲听到儿子叫门，高兴得来不及穿衣，披着毯子，拖鞋也穿错了脚，冲出来开门，杨黼见了立刻大悟。
In her joyful haste to greet her returning son, YangFu's mother threw on a blanket and accidentally put her slippers in the wrong feet. As she reshed out the door to meet him, Yang Fu took one look at her and was suddenly enlightened.

6

发自内心的善念常能使我们挣脱小我的躯壳，它像蛙声一样，使我们能够大彻大悟。
A wholesome thought from within the mind can often help us slough off the shell of our inferior selves and, like the croak of a frog, cause a sudden and profound enlightenment.

21

迷途的学子
The Lost
Student

1
盘珪和尚在一次静修会中对弟子讲道……
One day while the Zen master Bankei was giving a lecture, a disciple suddenly stood up and yelled out...

又抓到你偷钱了!
Ah ha! Caught you filching money again!

可恶!
What a shame!

2
原谅他吧!
Forgive him!

3
不行! 他已经行窃很多次了，这次不能再原谅他了。
No way! We've forgiven him every time, and he just keeps on stealing.

如果不把他开除，我们就集体离开这里。
Yea! If you don't kick him out this time, we'll all leave.

4
你们都是明智的师兄，知道是非。但他却连是非都分不清，如果我不教他谁来教他?
You are all perceptive students and understand the difference between right and wrong. He is the only one who doesn't understand even this. If I don't teach him, who will?

我要把他留在这里，即使你们全都离开也是一样。
I am going to let him stay here, even if every one of you leaves.

如果你有一百只羊，走失了一只，你会急忙地到处去寻找走失的那一只，而把其他九十九只撇在旷野吗? 去帮助最需要帮助的吧。
If you had one hundred sheep and one of them lost its way, wouldn't you immediately go in search of the lost one, abandoning the other ninety-nine in the open fields? It is important to help those who need help the most.

5
听了这话……偷窃的那位和尚跪倒在地，从此洗心革面悟出是非善恶了。
At this, the pick-pocket monk fell to his knees and promised to reform, suddenly understanding right and wrong, good and bad.

强盗的觉悟
Enlightenment
of the Thief

1 有个强盗抢劫七里禅师。
A thief once went to rob the Zen master Shichiri!

钱拿出来，不然就要你的老命。
Give me your money or I'll take your life!

2 钱在抽屉里，你自己拿，但留一点给我买食物。
My money's in the dresser over there, you may help yourself. I'd appreciate it, though, if you'd leave a little behind for me to buy food.

3 收了别人的东西应该说声谢谢啊！
After receiving something from someone, you should say thank you.

谢谢。
Thank you.

4 后来这个强盗被捕了……
A few days later, the thief was apprehended...

他抢了你的钱吗？
Did this man steal your money?

5 他没向我抢，钱是我给他的，他也谢过我了。
Oh no, he didn't steal it, I gave it to him. He even thanked me for it.

6 这个人服刑期满之后，立刻来叩见七里禅师，求他收自己为徒弟。
After serving a prison term for other crimes, the thief immediately returned to Shichiri, begging to be accepted as his disciple.

"放下屠刀立地成佛"是很难做到的，是什么力量使人放下屠刀？"爱心"罢了！
"Laying down his butcher's knife, he became a Buddha." This is a most difficult thing to do, and what is it that can get people to lay down their butcher's knives? Love-that's all.

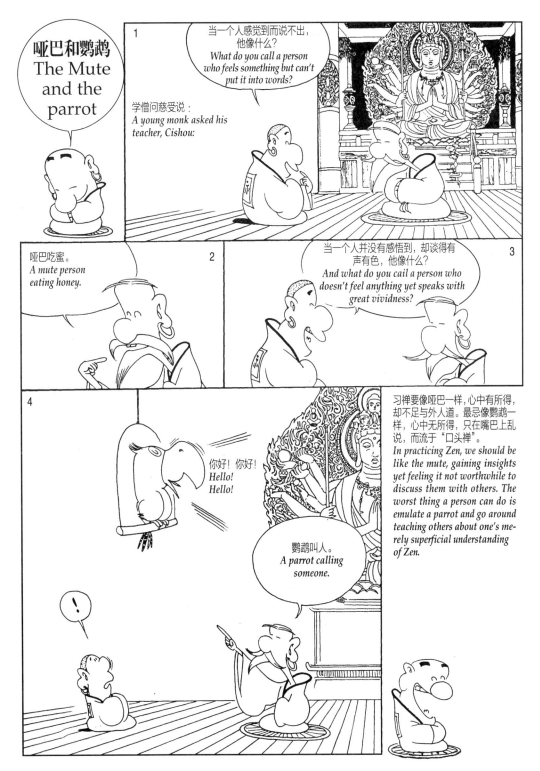

哑巴和鹦鹉
The Mute
and the
parrot

1

当一个人感觉到而说不出，他像什么？
What do you call a person who feels something but can't put it into words?

学僧问慈受说：
A young monk asked his teacher, Cishou:

2

哑巴吃蜜。
A mute person eating honey.

3

当一个人并没有感悟到，却谈得有声有色，他像什么？
And what do you call a person who doesn't feel anything yet speaks with great vividness?

4

你好! 你好!
Hello! Hello!

鹦鹉叫人。
A parrot calling someone.

习禅要像哑巴一样，心中有所得，却不足与外人道。最忌像鹦鹉一样，心中无所得，只在嘴巴上乱说，而流于"口头禅"。
In practicing Zen, we should be like the mute, gaining insights yet feeling it not worthwhile to discuss them with others. The worst thing a person can do is emulate a parrot and go around teaching others about one's merely superficial understanding of Zen.

25

茶杯禅理
Zen in
a Cup

一休禅师有一天打破了一个茶杯，这个茶杯是他师父非常喜爱的稀世之宝。
The Zen master Kasyapa had always been very clever. One day as a yiung monk, he got himself into trouble by accidentally breaking his master's favorite teacup.

哎呀!
Oh no!

1

2
咳!
Ahem.

3
师父，
人为什么一定要死呢?
Master, why must people die?

4
这是自然的事，世间的一切，有生就有死。
It's natural, my son. Everything in this world experiences both life and death.

5
老师! 你的茶杯死期到了。
Master, death has come upon your teacup.

6
嘻嘻!
Hee, hee, hee!

!

人生最可贵的是"生"的过程，有生自然会有死，能看透人的生死，自然也能看透物的生死。
The process of life is the most precious thing we have. If there is life, then naturally there will be death. If we can see through our own mortality, then surely we can see through the mortality of material objects.

不识头衔
Disre-gar-
ding
Titles

大将军北垣与东福寺住持是多年的朋友。
One day, the great general Kitagaki went to see his old pal, who was the abbot of Tofuku Temple.

1
大将军北垣求见！
The great general Kitagaki seeks an audience.

我不认识什么大将军。
I don't know any great generals.

2

师父请你回去，因为他不认识什么大将军。
The master said he can't see you. He doesn't know any great generals.

3

烦请再通报一次，是北垣求见！
Oh, I'm sorry.Please go back and tell him it's Kitagaki that's here to see him!

好吧！我再试试看。
Ok, I'll give it a try.

4

啊！是北垣啊！请到里面坐。
Ah! Kitagaki, please come in.

5

名、地位、成就、财富常常会蒙蔽了里面的那个真实的"我"。于是人常像游子迷了路回不了家一样。
Name, position, achievements, and wealth often conceal the real "self" inside, making one feel like a traveler who can't find his way home.

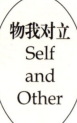

物我对立
Self
and
Other

有位军医，随着军队出征打仗，在战场上救治伤兵……
There was a certain army doctor, whose job it was to accompany soldiers to battle and tend to their wounds on the battlefield...

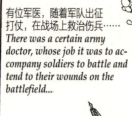

1

2

他的病人方愈，即又投入战场继续作战，于是再次伤亡……
But it seemed like every time he patched someone up, the soldier would just go right back into battle and end up being killed...

3

这种情况往复多次后，他终于崩溃了……
After this had happened over and over again, the doctor finally broke down...

4

如果他命中注定要死，我何必将他救活？如果我的医疗是有意义的，那么他为何又去战死呢？
If it's their fate to die, why should I try to save them? If my medicine means anything, then why do they go back to war and get killed?

28

5
他不明白当军医有何意义，心里乱得无法继续行医……
Not understanding what significance there was in being an army doctor, he felt extremely confused and couldn't go on with his work...

6
于是他即到山上找了一位禅师。
So he went into the mountains in search of a Zen master.

7
跟随禅师几个月后……
After studying with the Zen master for several months...

8
终于他想通了问题，又再次下山行医，他说：
He finally understood his problem and descended the mountain to continue his practice. When troubled with doubts thereafter, he simply said:

9
因为我就是医生啊！
Because I'm a doctor!

不把自我放到所接触的事物中去，也不把事物和自我对立，故无所谓主观，也无所谓客观，无我无相而法相宛然，才是智慧的领域。
Don't project your self on things you come into contact with, and don't differentiate between yourself and other things, because socalled subjectivity and objectivity do wisdom is in understanding that there is no self, there is no other, and everything is the way it is.

言过其行
Words Exceeding Actions

1
我年纪已经一大把了，您什么时候来接我都行，南无阿弥陀佛。
I've lied a long life, and I am ready whenever you would like to come for me. Praise to Amitabba.

有位富有的老太太，她经常到庙里供香，每次在佛前顶礼时都说：
There was once a wealthy old woman who often went to the temple to burn incense and pray. Kneeling in front of the buddha, she would always say:

我年纪已经一大把了，您什么时候来接我都行，南无阿弥陀佛。
I've lived a long life, and I am ready whenever you would like to come for me. Praise to Amitabha.

老太太，那么今晚请你来吧。
Old woman, tonight is the night.

嘻嘻。
Hee hee.

捉弄她一下。
Let's have some fun with her.

2

3

4

结果，这老太太竟被吓死了。
The old woman was terribly frightened by this and died right there from the shock.

哇！
Oh no!

色彩动人的言辞，会失去质朴，招致散乱。唯有言行一致，才是一切修行的基础。
Colorful and inspiring words will lose their simplicity and cause confusion. Consistency between actions and words in the foundation of self-cultivation.

5

30

命运在自己手里
Fate is in
Your Own
Hands

1 古时候，有一位将军率军要与实力比他强十倍的敌人打仗。
In ancient times, there was a general who was about to lead his troops into battle against an enemy army ten times the size of his own.

带队前进的途中，他下马向路边小庙朝拜祷告……
Along the way, he stopped at a small roadside altar to pray...

2

3 现在我投钱问卜。如果正面朝上表示我们会赢，朝下表示我们会输。
I'm now going to use this coin to predict our fate. If it's heads, we'll win. If it's tails, we'll lose.

4 我们的命运握在神的手里！
Our fate is in the hands of the gods!

5 锵 Kink

哇！正面朝上！
Hey! It's heads!

我们会赢！
We're going to win!

快出发去把敌人干掉！
Let's go get'em!

赢定了！
We'll crush'em!

6

决战之下，他们果然把强大的敌军打败了。
The battle commenced, and just as predicted, the smaller army defeated the larger army.

7

8

神的决定，谁也不能改变。
No one can change a fate determined by the gods.

天对万物全部一视同仁，并不会特别帮助任何一个人的。能帮助你的，只是你自己而已。
Heaven looks on all beings just the same and won't help anyone in particular. The one who can help you is yourself.

9

是吗？
Is that right?

将军拿出问卜的硬币，两面都是正面。
The general reached into his pocket and pulled out the coin, both sides of which were heads.

越急越慢
The Faster the Slower

1 有一位少年，到山上请一位异人传授剑法。
An eager student ascended the mountains to study the art of swordfighting under a great master.

师父，假如我努力学习，需要多久才能学成？
Master, if I study diligently, how long will it take me to learn the skills of swordfighting?

也许十年吧。
Ten years, perhaps.

2

家父年事渐高，我得服侍他，假如我更加刻苦学习，需要多久才能学成？
My father is an old man, and I must return to look after him. What if I work exceptionally hard, then how long will it take me?

嗯，这样大概要三十年。
Um, in that case, it will probably take thirty years.

3 4

你先说十年而现在又说三十年……我不惜任何劳苦，一定要在最短的时间内学成。
First you said ten years and now you say thirty... Look, I'm willing to suffer any kind of hardship and sacrifice. I just want to learn it in the shortest time possible.

这样得跟我学七十年才能学成。
In that case, you'll have to study with me for seventy years.

急功近利的人多半是欲速则不达，"平常心是道"正是这个道理。
If we take our time, we'll achieve our goals faster than if we hurry. This is what is meant by, "The ordinary mind is the Dao".

5 6

将军的古玩
The General's Antique

1
有一位将军，在家中把玩他所珍藏的古玩……
A general was at home admiring a certain antique that was very precious to him...

2
哎呀!
Oh no!

我带领千万大军，出生入死都未曾害怕过，为何今天为一只杯子就惊吓成这个样子?
I've led thousands of men into battle, and I've neverbeen afraid in the face of death. why was I so frightened today by this little cup?

3
好险!
Whew! That was close.

4

5
终于他悟通了，有了爱憎之心才使他惊骇，于是他随手就把杯子摔碎了。
Finally, the general realized that it was his differentiating "like" and "dislike" in his mind that led to his being frightened. Upon realizing this, he tossed the cup over his shoulder, smashing it to pieces.

有了得失之志，有了得失之心，就有了悲欢喜乐。应该要超越善恶、得失，随缘即是福。
Being concerned with gain and loss brings us the feelings of happiness and sadness. We should transcend the concepts of good anbd evil, gain and loss. Happiness is acting according to circumstances, whatever they may be.

施与受
Giving
and
Receiving

1. 我老了，此书极有价值，现在交给你表示你的继承。
I'm getting old. Top symbolize your succeding me, I give you this precious book.

2. 我接受你不立文字的禅，我喜欢它的本来面目。这本书你还是自己保存吧。
No, no no. I have accepted your Zen that is not teliant on the written word. I like its original face. You go ahead and keep the book.

3. 这本书已传了七代，你还是拿去，作为承受衣钵的标记。
This book has been passed down for seven generations. You should still take it as a token of your accepting the robe and alms bowl.

好吧。
All right.

4. ！

5. 你在干什么？
What are you doing?

6. 你在说什么？
What are you saying?

知与行应合而为一，讲学而不身体力行，正如不懂佛理而只会念经的口头禅。
Knowledge and action should be one. Preaching something but not practicing it is just like someone who recites the scriptures but doesn't understand the principles of Buddhism.

知音人
One Who Understands the Music

1

伯牙擅长鼓琴，钟子期善于听琴音。
Bo Ya was an excellent zither player, and Zhong Ziqi loved nothing more that to listen to him play.

2

每当伯牙弹高山之歌时……
When Bo Ya played a majestic song, Zhong Ziqi saw it as it was...

好美哦，像泰山一样高壮！
Wow, it's as majestic as Mount Tai!

3

而当伯牙奏出流水之曲时……
And when Bo Ya played a relaxed, flowing tune...

好美哦！像长江黄河一样悠长。
Wow, it's long and leisurely like the Yangtze and Yellow rivers.

4

后来，钟子期病死了，伯牙也从此不再弹琴了。
Then one day, Zhong Ziqi became ill and died. After this, Bo Ya never played the zither again.

伯牙把琴弦割断。自那以后，"断弦"便象征着知音的丧失。
IIn fact, he went home and took a knife to its strings. Henceforward, "broken strings" came to signify the death of one's closest friend.

5

知音难寻，知音人死了，伯牙虽然是活生生的一个人，其实只剩下半个了。
A person who understands one's music is difficult to find. When the person who understood his music died, although Bo Ya was still very much alive, only half of hin remained.

37

值钱的东西
Something Valuable

1 有一个小偷到良宽禅师的茅庐偷东西，结果发现没有一样值钱的东西。
One day, a thief entered the hut of the Zen master Ryokan, but he discovered that there wasn't anything worth stealing.

2

3 你远道而来，不该让你空手而回，这件衣服你带走吧。
You've come such a long way, I wouldn't want you to go home empty-handed. Here, take this piece of clothing.

4

5

可怜的家伙，可惜我不能把这美丽的月亮也送给他。
Poor guy. If only I could give him this beautiful moon as well.

一般人只追求名利，其实天地之间你拥有的何其多？星、月、山、水，一花一草都因你而在！
Most people pursue only fame and fortune, but think of how much there is in nature that you stars, the moon, mountains, rivers, flowers, and trees all because of you!

39

一株草一点露
A Blade of Grass, a Drop of Dew

1
行行行，这样刚刚好。
Mmm... there, that's perfect.

仪山禅师洗澡时，因为水太热，叫弟子用冷水冲凉一些……
One day while the Zen master Yishan was taking his bath, his bath water was too hot, so he asked a disciple to add a little cold water...

2
!

3
笨蛋！大小事物各有用处，何不活用？给树树也欢喜，水也活着。
You idiot! Everything big and small has its use. Why did you waste that? You could at least dump it by a tree. A tree would welcome it, and the water would be put to good use.

4
何不拿去浇浇花草？你为何要浪费寺里的一滴水？
Why didn't you dump it in the flower bed? Why must you waste even one drop of the monastery's water?

5
小和尚因此而开悟了，于是他取法号为"滴水和尚"。
This scolding brought the monk to enlightenment, and from that day forward, he went by the name, "Drop of Water".

万物皆有所用，无论多么的卑微，都有自己的一片天空、自己的一席之地。
Everything has its own use. Regardless of some things' seeming insignificance, everything has its place in nature.

不为任何
For No
Reason

1
那个人站在山上干什么？
What's that guy doing on the mountain over there?

去问问他。
Let's go ask him.

2
你站在这里等朋友吗？
Are you standing here waiting for a friend?

不是。
No.

3
那么是为了呼吸新鲜空气？
Then you're here to breath the fresh air, right?

不是。
No.

4
是站在这里看风景吗？
Are you here to take in the beautiful scenery?

不是。
No.

5
既然什么都不是，那么你为什么站在这里？
Then why are you standing here?

6
我只是在这儿站着。
I'm just here standing.

一般人都活在"二元世界"里，于是就有得失。"我和对象"，对象景色美，我愉快；景色不美，我失望。
Most people live in a dualistic world of gains and losses, self and object. If the scenery is beautiful, I'm happy; if it's not, I'm disappointed.

41

過去，現在，未來
Past, Present, Future

1
有一个人在荒郊遇到一只老虎……
One day while walking through the wilderness, a man happened upon a vicious tiger.

救命啊！
Au secours!

2
他跑到一处悬崖，双手攀着野藤，只见老虎仍在下面张口怒吼……
He ran but soon came to the edge of a cliff. Climbing down a vine, he discovered another tiger at the bottom...

3
又见一只白鼠和一只黑鼠正在上面啃噬枯藤……
Then two rats aooeared and began gnawing on the vine...

4
裂！
Rip!

Oh non...

5
忽然他看见一棵鲜美的草莓。
Suddenly, he noticed a plump red strawberry.

6
于是他将草莓送入口中……
He plucked it and popped it in his mouth...

味道好美啊！
Delicious!

不思过去，不想将来，体验珍惜即刻，随缘即是福。
Don't dwell on the past. Don't worry about the future. Experience and cherish the moment. Happiness is acting according to circumstances, whatever they may be.

心中的大浪
The Great Wave

有一位名叫大波的摔跤高手，他不但体格强壮，而且精于摔跤之道。
There was once a wrestler named Dapo (great wave), who was not only big and strong, but was also highly skilled in wrestling.

在私下较量时，他厉害非凡，连他的老师都不是他的对手。
During practice, he was unbeatable, out-wrestling even his teacher.

但在正式比赛时，他却腼腆得连他的徒弟都打不过……
But during matches, he couldn't beat even the puniest of students...

啊！
Oh!

于是，他只好到深山求教禅师。
Not knowing what else to do, he went into the hills in search of a Zen master.

你叫大波，那么你就想象自己是巨大的波浪，能横扫一切、吞噬一切的狂涛巨浪，而不是个怯场的摔跤手。
Your name means great wave, right? So imagine that you are a massive tidal wave demolishing everything in your path, instead of a weenie wrestler suffering from stage fright.

你只要如此做，不久就会成为全国最伟大的摔跤手，没有一个人可以打败你了。
Do this, and in no time you will be the greatest wrestler in the nation—invincible.

是。
Yes, master.

43

于是大波就在寺里打坐，尝试把自己想象成巨浪。起初他杂念纷飞，但不久……
So Dapo remained in the temple and meditated, imagining that he was a giant wave. At first, he had difficulty concentrating, but after a while...

他对波浪愈来愈有感应了……
Waves began rolling in ...

夜深了，波浪愈来愈大，波浪卷走了花瓶、佛具……
And as the night went on, the waves became larger and larger, until they knocked over vases and carried away items of worship...

12

浪淹没了佛像，淹没了佛堂……
They overwhelmed statues and flooded the temple...

13

海潮腾涌，最后连佛寺也整座被淹没得看不见了……
Then the tide came in, and the entire temple was swept away...

醒醒！你终于办到了。
Wake up, wake up! You've done it.

!

现在什么也不能烦恼你了，你可以像波浪一样横扫一切。
Now nothing will bother you. You can be like a tidal wave demolishing everything in its path.

谢谢师父。
Thenk you, master.

14

15

从此大波比赛时就把自己想象成波浪，他成了全国最厉害的高手，没有人能打败他。
In his matches thereafter, Dapo imagined that he turned into a wave, and he became the greatest wrestler in the nation—invincible.

16

只要以一种绝对直接的方式去反映某个情境，你就会变成那个情境，而那个情境也就变成你了。
All you have to do is respond in a direct, resolute way to any situation, and you will become that situation, and that situation will become you.

因为我在
Because
I'm Here

1　有位年纪很大的老和尚在烈日下晒菜干……
An old monk was drying vegetables under the scorching sun...

2　你今年高寿了？
How old are you?

六十八。
Sixty-eight.

3　为什么还要这么辛苦地在这里工作？
Why are you still working so hard here?

4　因为我在这里。
Because I'm here.

因为太阳在这里。
Because the sun is there.

5　但也没必要在大太阳底下工作啊？
But why are you working under the hot sun?

6　天地日月恩泽万物，但却为而不恃，功成而不倨。人勤劳地工作而不抱怨，乃是与天地日月结合为一。
Heaven and earth nurture all things, but we should act without counting on the results and strive for success without dwelling on it. If we just work hard without complaining, we can become one with heaven and earth.

46

色即是空
Matter
is
Empty

请你画出"直指人心，见性成佛"这种境界的"心"。
Paint me a scene depicting the saying, "Direct pointing at one's mind, Seeing one's nature, becoming the Buddha."

益中和尚是个有名的画家……
There was once a monk named Yi Zhong who was a famous painter.

直指人心
见性成佛

1

好。
Ok.

2

你干什么？！
What are you doing?!

3

画好了，这就是"心"。
It's done. This is "mind".

4

"见性成佛"的"性"是不是也能画出来瞧瞧？
And can you paint "nature", as well?

5

你先拿出"性"来让我瞧瞧，我就替你画。
Sure. You hand over "nature," and I'll paint it for you.

6

自性是一切具足，没有欠缺的，每个人的自性要靠自己去发现，因为没有别的路可以从外面通向我们的自性。
Your self-nature is complete and undiminished. We must all discover our self-nature on our own because there is no external road that can take us there.

成佛成魔
一念间
The
Weeping
Lady

有一位绰号"哭婆"的老婆婆，她不但下雨时哭，晴天她也哭……
There was once an old woman who was known as the "Weeping Lady" because she cried all the time. On rainy days she would cry, and on clear days she would cry...

老婆婆, 你为什么哭呢？
Old lady, why are you crying all the time?

因为我有两个女儿, 大女儿嫁给卖鞋的, 小女儿嫁给卖伞的。
Because I diaughters-one who married a shoe salesman and one who married an umbrella salesman.

天气好的日子, 我就想到小女儿的雨伞一定卖不出去。
On days when the weather is good, I think of how my daughter's umbrella business is bad.

下雨的日子, 我就想到大女儿, 雨天一定不会有顾客上门啊！
And on rainy days, I think of how no one will go out to buy shoes from my other daughter!

你应晴天时想到大女儿的店生意会很好, 雨天时小女儿的伞一定卖得好啊！
But on clear days, you should think of how good your daughter's shoe business is; and on rainy days, you should think of how good your other daughter's umbrella business is!

啊! 对！
Hey, you're right!

从此, 好哭的婆婆再也不哭了, 无论晴天、雨天总是笑嘻嘻的。
From that day on, the Weeping Lady wept no more. Instead, she chuckled to herself everyday regardless of the weather.

"即心即佛", 一样事情的发生, 是喜？是忧？全在于你是站在哪一个角度去看它！
If "the mind is the Buddha," then whether a situation is good or bad all depends on how you look at the situation!

山径不变
Mountain Paths Don't Change

1 有位将军，他经常在战役中奋勇杀敌。
There was once a general who fought wars with utmost bravery and courage.

2 他年老时，因感于世事变化无常而遁入佛门。
When he became older, he was troubled over the constant changes in the world; so he turned to Buddhism.

3

4 常有人问他为何改变，他回答说：
After studying for some time, people would often ask him why things change; and he would answer...

山和山径是万难改变的，变的是我的心。
Mountains and mountain paths never change, it's our minds that change.

5 至人用心若镜，不将不迎，应而不藏。所以应做到当将军时当将军，做和尚时做和尚。
The perfect person's mind is like a mirror, neither taking nor welcoming, it responds but doesn't store. So, when it's time to be a general, you should be a general, and when it's time to be a monk, be a monk.

违顺相争
是为心病
Torn

慧春尼姑长得很美，在一次禅会中有一个和尚偷偷地爱上她……
There was once a nun named Eshun who was very beautiful, and one day during a lecture, a young monk secretly fell in love with her...

啊？
Huh?

和尚还写了一封情书，要求一次私下的约会。
He wrote her a love letter, in which he said that he wanted to meet with her in private.

第二天，禅师说法既罢，慧春站起来对着写信给她的和尚说：
The next day, as soon as the master ended his lecture, Eshun stood up and said to the monk who wrote the letter:

如果你真的那样爱我，现在就来拥抱我啊！
If you really love me, then come up here right now and embrace me!

内心如果夹缠着两种概念，就会因矛盾而破坏了内心的统一、安详。所以应该要当取即取、当舍即舍。
If your mind is torn by two conflicting desires, the contradiction will destroy your mind's unity and tranquillity. Just remember, when you should grab something, grab it; when you should let go, let go.

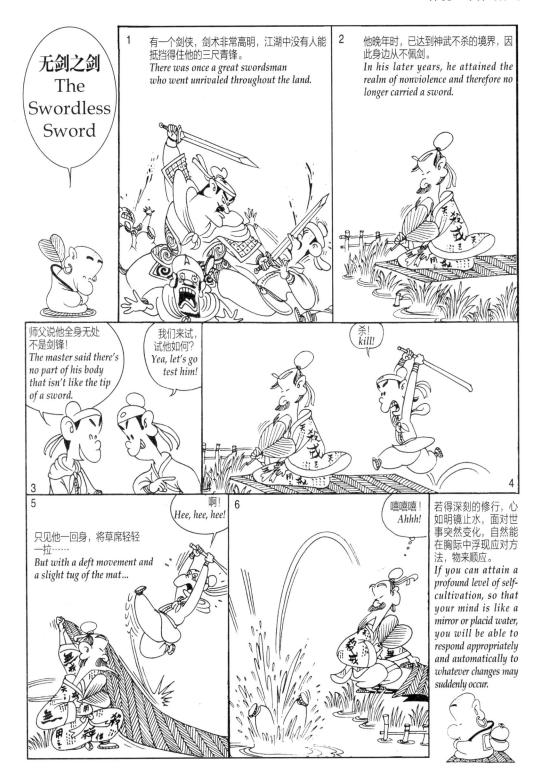

无剑之剑
The Swordless Sword

1　有一个剑侠，剑术非常高明，江湖中没有人能抵挡得住他的三尺青锋。
There was once a great swordsman who went unrivaled throughout the land.

2　他晚年时，已达到神武不杀的境界，因此身边从不佩剑。
In his later years, he attained the realm of nonviolence and therefore no longer carried a sword.

3　师父说他全身无处不是剑锋。
The master said there's no part of his body that isn't like the tip of a sword.

我们来试，试他如何？
Yea, let's go test him!

杀！
Kill!

4

5　只见他一回身，将草席轻轻一拉……
But with a deft movement and a slight tug of the mat...

啊！
Hee, hee, hee!

6　嘻嘻嘻！
Ahhh!

若得深刻的修行，心如明镜止水，面对世事突然变化，自然能在胸际中浮现应对方法，物来顺应。
If you can attain a profound level of self-cultivation, so that your mind is like a mirror or placid water, you will be able to respond appropriately and automatically to whatever changes may suddenly occur.

53

轻轻一拨扇，
炉火又起焰
With a slight
Fanning, the
Fire Returns

大慧果禅师在山林里修行，有位退役将军有意追随他出家……
One day when the Zen master Dahui Zonggao was in the mountains meditating, a retired general approached and informed Dahui of his intent to become a monk...

等我将自身的坏习惯除尽，再来追随师父。
As soon as I eliminate my bad habits, I'll return to become your disciple.

好。
Fine.

师父，我已经除却心头心，特来参喜禅。
Master, I'm ready now. I've rid myself of all my bad habits.

缘何起得早，妻与他入眠。
Why did yor get up so early? Your wife is home sleeping with another man.

何方僧秃子，焉敢乱开言？
You bald-headed moron! How dare you?!

出家还早得很呢，回去再修几年方可出家。
I think it's a little early for you to become a monk. You'd better run along home and practice more self-control.

言与行，是人的内在思想表现于外在的两面；但一般人却往往言过其行，甚至言而不行！
Words and actions are two exterior manifestations of our inner thoughts; but most people's words exceed their actions, even to the point of there being no action at all!

54

魔由心生
The Spider and the Monk

1 有位和尚，每次入定都遇到一只大蜘蛛来跟他捣蛋。
There was once a monk who was bothered by a great big spider whenever he tried to meditate.

嘅......
Hmm...

2 我一入定，大蜘蛛就出现了，无论我怎么赶它，它也不走。
Every time I meditate, this big spider appears, and no matter what I do, I just can't get rid of him.

3 下次你入定时，拿一支笔，如果蜘蛛再来，你就在它的肚子上画一个圈圈做记号，看看它是何方的怪物。
Next time you go to meditate, grab a brush, and if that spider shows up again, draw a circle right on its belly; then you will see what kind of a monster it is.

是。
Ok.

4 和尚照办了，当他在蜘蛛的肚子上画了圈圈后，蜘蛛就走了，他也安然入定。
So the monk took his master's advice, and as soon as he had finished drawing the circle on the spider's belly, the spider disappeared and the monk was able to continue meditating in peace.

5 待出定，一看赫然发现，那个圈圈在他自己的肚子上。
When he withdrew from his concentration, the first thing he saw was a big, black circle right on his own belly.

嘻嘻
Hee hee!

人生中往往会遭遇到很多的困扰与烦恼，其中最大的困扰往往是来自于自己！
We all experience troubles and worries, but it often happens that our greatest troubles arise from ourselves!

55

贫与富
Rich and Poor

1
哇! 金罗汉!
Wow! A golden arhat!

有一农夫, 在山野中挖到一尊价值连城的金罗汉。
There was once a farmer who discovered a priceless statue of one of the eighteen Buddhist arhats(holy men) on a hillside in a forest.

差不多一百多斤的金子打造的呢。
That's gotta be a hundred pounds of pure gold!

哈哈哈, 我们这一生都可吃喝不尽了!
Ha, ha! We'll have enough to eat and drink forever!

他的家人和亲友都很为他高兴。
The farmer's family and friends were all very excited about the find.

3
可是农夫却闷闷不乐, 整天愁眉苦脸的坐着沉思……
But the farmer felt dejected and just sat around with a worried look on his face...

4
忧愁啊……
Wor-ried about...

你已成千万富翁了, 还有什么事好忧愁的呢?
You're a wealthy man, now. What are you so worried about?

5
因为我不知道另外的十七座罗汉在哪里?
Why, I still don't know where the other seventeen arhats are!

富不富有, 不在于金钱的多寡, 而在于知足不知足。
Rich and poor are not functions of how much money we have, but rather, of whether or not we are content with what we have.

56

不执着两边
Do Not
Grasp Either
Extreme

1. 有一个富人，他虽然非常有钱，但生性吝啬，从来都舍不得花一文钱。
There was once a very wealthy man who was so miserly that he couldn't bear to spend even a single cent of his vast wealth.

2. 有一天，默仙禅师来拜访他……
One day, the Zen master Mokusen paid him a visit...

3. 畸形。
Deformed.

假如我的拳头永远这样始终不变，你称那叫什么？
If I held my hand in a fist like this forever, what would you call it?

还不是一样，畸形！
The same, deformed!

4. 假如这只手永远这样，始终不变，你又称它做什么？
And if I opened it up like this and kept it this way forever, what would you call it?

5. 只要你能了解这点，你就是个快乐的有钱人。
As long as you understand this, you'll be a happy rich man.

一切相对的好恶、有无、利害、人我等等，都是分别心。才一起见便背本心，就落在两边，而禅是中亦不立的。
All opposites-good and evil, having and lacking, benefit and harm, self and others—are due to the differentiating mind. As soon as we give rise to such views, we turn away from our original mind and succumb to this dualism. Zen, however, stands in the middle, not on either side.

6. 从此，这位富人就变得很通达，不仅节俭也懂得施舍、花钱。
From that day forward, the wealthy man became a generous man. He was still frugal, but he also understood how to spend money and contribute to charities.

不变应万变
Not Changing to Meet the Changes

有两座禅院比邻而居，各有一名小沙弥；其中的一个每晨到市场买菜时，总会碰到另一个。
There were once two neighboring Zen monasteries, each with a young novice. Every morning on his way to the market, one novice would run into the other.

1

2

你要到哪里去？
Where are you going?

脚到哪里，我到哪里。
Wherever my feet take me.

3

下次他仍这样回答时，你就问他："如果没有脚你到哪里？"
Next time ask him, "What if you had no feet?"

4

这下他定回答不了。
Yea, that'll get him.

5

你要到哪里去？
Where are you going?

天地同笑
Laughing with heaven and Earth

有一天晚上，药山和尚登山经行，
The great Zen master Weiyan of Yaoshan, like many well-known Zen masters, came to be identified by his place of residence, and so we call him Yaoshan. One evening, Yaoshan went for a walk in the hills.

突然云雾大开，看见月亮，药山不禁哈哈大笑。
Suddenly, the clouds and fog parted, and the moon could be seen shining brightly in the sky. On seeing this, Yaoshan let out a hearty laugh.

哈哈哈！
Ha, ha, ha!

笑声传到十公里以外还听得到。
It was so loud that it could be heard for miles in all directions.

昨夜突然传来一阵笑声，不知是从哪里来的？
Las night, I suddenly heard a laughing sound, but i have no idea where it could have come from?

是啊！
我也听到了。
Yes, I heard it, too.

那是我们老师昨夜在山顶上大笑的声音。
That was the sound of our master laughing in the hills.

人在任何场合中，只要忘我便能与境合而为一；药山的忘我大笑，便和天地合为一体。
If we can just forget our selves, we can become one with our environment no matter what the circumstances. Yaoshan was able to forget himself and laugh out loud, thus becoming one with heaven and earth.

禅不可说
Zen Can't Be Spoken

1
药山禅师很久不升座说法。
It had been quite a while since Yaoshan had given a lecture.

弟子似都很希望能听师父的示诲。
All of the disciples seem very eager to receive the master's guidance.

好吧！去打钟叫大家到大殿听法。
O.k., ring the bell, and have everyone gather in the temple hall.

2
咚咚咚 Dong, dong, dong

3

4

5
师父你为什么一句话也没说就走了呢？
Master, why are you leaving without saying anything?

6
讲经有讲经的法师，说戒有说戒的律师，我是禅师，而禅是不能讲的，讲了也没有用。这怎能怪我呢？
There are dharma teachers to teach the sutras, and there are disciplinarians to teach the prohibitions, but I'm a Zan teacher. It's no use talking about it because Zen can't be put into words. So how can you blame me?

"禅" 不属于过去、现在、未来。它是本来如此，是言语所不能表达的。
Zen belongs to neither the past, the present, nor the future. It has just always been the way it is, and it can't be expressed through words.

云在青天水在瓶
Clouds in the Blue Sky, Water in a Bottle

文豪李翱来拜见药山，药山正在念经没有回头看李翱……
The famous scholar Li Ao once paid a visit to Yaoshan, but at the time, Yaoshan was busy reciting scriptures and so paid no heed to his visitor...

与其见面，还不如闻名来得好。
Hmph! Hearing about him was actually more interesting than seeing him.

李居士！
Mister Li!

你相信你的耳朵，却轻视你的眼睛。
You believe your ears but underestimate your eyes.

抱歉失礼了，请师父原谅。
Please forgive my impertinence.

法师，你认为什么才算是道？
Master, what is the Dao?

云在青天上，水在水瓶中。
Clouds in the blue sky, and water in a bottle.

不必去计较云将变成水，或水将变回云；是云就以云的立场在天空逍遥，是水就以水的立场安逸自在。
Don't worry about whether the clouds are going to turn into water or whether the water is going to turn into clouds. If it's clouds, take a cloud's leisurely point of view, and if it's water, take water's placid, carefree point of view.

**好雪片片
不落别处
Snowflakes
fall Where
They Should**

庞居士访药山和尚，告辞时，药山请禅客送他出门。
A lay Buddhist by the name of Pang once paid a visit to Yaoshan. As he was about to leave, Yaoshan asked two of the monastery's guests to show him out.

你们替我送客吧。
Please show him out.

是。
Yes Sir.

好雪片片，每片都落到该落的位置。
Ah, look at the good snowflakes, each falling in its rightful place.

落到哪里？
And where might that be?

像你这样"眼明而瞎；能言而哑"也敢称禅客？
Look at you! Your eyes see like a blind man and your mouth speaks like a mute! You call yourself a student of Zen?

天下万物，无论巨细贵贱，皆有其容身处，各有各的位置，恰到好处，若问为何？本来如此！
Everything under heaven, whether it be large or small, important or insignificant, has its own particular place. And when it arrives in its rightful place, why ask why? That's just how it is!

63

赵州石桥
Zhaozhou's
Stone Bridge

传闻河北观音院有座非常有名的赵州石桥……
It had been said that near the Guanyin Monastery in Hebei province, there was a famous bridge called the Zhaozhou (Chao-chou) Stone Bridge...

1

听说这里有座赵州石桥，但我却只看到一座独木桥而已，石桥在哪里？
I have heard say of the Zhaozhou Stone Bridge, but when I arrived, all I saw was a bridge made out of a single log. Where's the stone bridge?

2

你只看到独木桥，却看不到赵州的石桥。
You only saw the single log, and you didn't see the stone bridge.

赵州的石桥到底是怎样的东西？
That's right. What exactly is Zhaozhou's stone bridge?

3

度驴度马度一切迷惘的众生。
It is the bridge that allows the crossing of donkeys, horses, and every confused being in the world.

4

有形的独木桥只度人一时，无形的赵州石桥却是以菩萨的慈悲心默默地以身承受驴马践踏，普度众生。
The actual single log bridge could let only one person cross at a time, but through the mercy of Zhaozhou, his abstract stone bridge allowed all beings to quietly cross at the same time.

洗钵去
Go Wash
Your Bowl

有一个人到观音院出家，并见了方丈赵州……
A man once went to Guanyin Monastery to become a monk and finally gained an audience with the abbot, Congshen of Zhaozhou (Zhaozhou for short)...

1

弟子第一次到这里来，请师父教我修行。
This is my first time here, and I'd appreciate it if the master could teach me about self-cultivation.

2

你吃过粥没有?
Have you eaten breakfast yet?

吃过了。
Yes, I have.

3

那么，先去把碗洗一洗。
Then go wash your bowl.

!

4

领悟、修行及日常行动都是属于同一件事情，要能够确认领悟到这种真实，并加以维持才是修行，而不是因为修行才能领悟。
Enlightenment, self-cultivation, and our daily activities are all parts of the same thing. It is essential to understand this fact of enlightenment, and it is the maintenance of this attitude that is self-cultivation. It is not because of self-cultivation that we gain enlightenment.

多归于一
The Many Return to One

宇宙万物的道理归于一，而这个一归向哪里？
All things return to one, but where does the one return to?

我在青州做了件布衫，重有七斤。
When I was in Qingzhou, I made a robe that weighed seven pounds.

宇宙万物虽分身百亿，各异其态，但其实还是宇宙本身。一和多是相即相融的，如果多归于一，那么一也归于多，因此宇宙中任何微小事物也都会归于一。
Although the universe is separated into an infinite number of parts, and each part has its own distinct identity, they are still all parts of one universal body, The one and the many interfuse with eachother, so if the many return to one, then the one returns to the many. Therefore, even the tiniest specks in the universe return to the one.

如何是
赵州?
What is
Zhao-
zhou?

赵州老年时，一直定居在赵州城外的观音院。
In his older years, Zhaozhou settled down in the Guanyin Monastery just outside the city of Zhaozhou.

1

什么是赵州？
What is
Zhaozhou?

2

东门，西门，南门，北门。
The eastern gate, the western gate, the southern gate, the northern gate.

3

赵州的禅风像赵州城门一样，四通八达，何处都可进入。有黄金皆可取走；要看，随便你来看个够。
Zhaozhou's Zen was just like the gates of Zhaozhou the city: approachable from all sides and leading in all directions. You could take what you wanted; and if you just wanted to look, you could do so to your heart's content.

庭前
柏树子
The
Cypress
Tree
Out
Front

1

什么是佛法，是大义？
What is the meaning of the Buddha-dharma?

庭前柏树子。
The cypress tree out front.

2

请别用物体来比喻。
Please don't use a metaphor involving concrete objects.

3

我并没有指物体啊。
Ok, I won't refer to anything concrete.

4

什么是佛法的大义？
So, what is the meaning of the Buddh-dharma?

5

庭前柏树子。
The cypress tree out front.

翠绿的山是清净的生命；溪水声如佛在说话，通过溪流声，柏树与全宇宙的生命产生共鸣并合而为一。
Gree mountains are pure life; a stream is the Buddha speaking—Through the sound of flowing water we see that the cypress tree resonates with the life of the universe, and they become one.

不持一物
Dropping Everything

我抛弃一切两手皆空，心中坦荡荡地来到这里。
I've dropped everything. My arms are empty and I come hither with a peaceful heart.

那么，放下来吧！
Then let go fo it.

我说连一物都没有，究竟要放下什么东西？
But I told you I've nothing. What else can I let go of?

那么你就带着吧！
Fine, then keep it!

不持一物就应连这个不持一物的观念也要舍弃，既然那么重视不持一物，那就永远无法达至清澄的心境。
Dropping everything must include casting aside the very idea of dropping everything. If you continually concentrate on dropping everything, you'll never reach that realm of purity and tranquillity.

吃茶去
Have Some Tea

德山宣鉴
Xuanjian of Deshan

四川剑南人，俗姓周。早岁出家，便博阅律藏、精通《金刚经》，时人都称他为周金刚。

后来他听到南方禅学很盛，便大为气愤不平，决心到南方挑战禅宗。

A native of Jiannan in Sichuan, Xuanjian's (Hsüan-chien) original surname was Zhou. He left home to join the monkhood at an early age and extensively studied the doctrines of discipline. He learned the entire Diamond Sutra by heart, and because of this he became known as Diamond Zhou.

Later, he learned that the rival Southern School of Zen had gained a great following. Inflamed by this, he headed south to challenge their teachings. His monastery was later located at Deshan (Te-shan) in Hunan province, so people refer to him as Deshan.

12 你已经到龙潭了。
You have arrived at Longtan.

我早向往龙潭，可是到了这里，潭也不见，龙也不现。
I planned on coming to see Longtan, but now that I've arrived, I see neither dragon nor pool.

德山只好饿着肚子直往龙潭。
With even the commoners thus enlightened, Deshan knew that there must be a great Zen master nearby. leaming of a master called Longtan (dragon-pool), Deshan went to see him.

13 德山默默无语，决心住下随侍在龙潭左右。
Deshan remained at the temple in silence, determined to learn what he could from Longtan.

14 夜已深了，回禅房睡觉吧。
It's late, perhaps you should go to your room and get some sleep.

是。
Yes, I should.

15 外面好黑哦！
Wow, look how dark it is!

16 我给你火……
Here's a candle...

17 呼！
Puff!

77

18

龙潭突然把烛光吹熄，就在这时，德山大悟。
Longtan suddenly blew out the candle, and it was at this time that Deshan Attained enlightenment.

第二天，德山把青龙疏钞在法堂上烧掉。
The next day, Deshan took his copy of the Qinglong Commentary to the main hall and burned it right there.

19

穷诸玄辩，若一毫置于太虚；竭世枢机，似一滴投于巨壑。
Learning all the various profound philosophies is like a mere strand of hair in the vasness of space; completely understanding the fundamental forces of the world is like a mere drop in a giant abyss.

当外在的光亮熄灭后，内在的光才射出了它的光辉；当依赖的对象失去后，自己的潜能才会被完全发挥。
It is not until the external light is extinguished that our internal light shines bright. It is not until our crutch is discarded that we can realize our latent potential.

20

临济宗的祖师临济义玄
Yixuan of Linji; Founder of the Linji School

临济是山东曹县人俗姓邢，幼年便立志出家，虔诚求道。二十岁左右，他到安徽投奔在黄檗门下。得道后，在河北镇州的临济禅院举扬一家的宗风。
Linji Yixuan (Lin-chi I-Hsüan) was a native of Cao County in Shandong province and his lay surname was Xing. While still a child, he decided to leave his family to become a monk, and he pursued the truth with great sincerity. Around the age of twenty, he went to Anhui province and studied under Huangbo. After attaining enlightenment, he settled down in Zhenzhou, Hebei province, and established the Lini Monastery, where he preached his own style of Zen.

临济常以"喝"接引学生，临济的用喝与德山的用棒齐名，而有"德山棒，临济喝"之称。
Linji often used the shout to induce enlightenment in his students, and his shout became likened to Deshan's use of the staff.

喝！The shout！　棒！The Staff！

也因此，临济的学生只知模仿学着喝，而并不知喝的作用和意思……
A side-effect of this practice was that Linji's students knew only how to imitate his use of the shout, but knew nothing of its function or its meaning...

喝！Ha！

投鞭断流
Cracking a Whip to Stop the Flow

有时一喝如金刚王宝剑，有时一喝如踞地狮子，有时一喝如探竿影草，有时一喝不作一喝用。
Sometimes a shout is like the precious sword of the Diamond-king; sometimes a shout is like a crouching golden-haired lion; sometimes a shout is like a fishing lure; sometimes a shout doesn't work like a shout at all.

一次，临济对一学僧说：
Linji once said to a student:

你了解吗？
Do you understand?

我……
I...

学僧正犹豫要回答，临济便喝。
And just as the student was preparing to answer, Linji let out a loud shout.

喝！ Ha!

把人我、内外、大小、好坏、迷悟、生死、有无等对立的观念全打消了，禅境与悟境才会出现，使你获得一个新的生命。而为寻求这境界，并不是用思维，是用自己的直观。
In order to attain the realm of Zen and enlightenment, you must first forsake the dualities of: self and others, interior and exterior, small and large, good and bad, delusion and enlightenment, life and death, being and nothingness. We can attain this new life not through thought, but through direct insight.

81

无依、无求
No Crutches, No Desires

1 有一天，临济去拜访达摩的纪念塔。
One day, Linji paid a visit to a pagoda built in memorial of Bodhidharma, the first patriarch of Zen in China.

你是先拜佛？还是先拜祖呢？
Which shall you pay reverence to first, Bodhidharma or the Buddha?

2 佛和祖，我都不拜！
I'll pay reverence to heither Bodhidharma nor the Buddha!

佛和祖，跟你究竟有什么冤仇啊？
And what have they done to you?

3 4

啊！
Oh!

临济即拂袖而去！
With a flourish of his robe, Linji had turned and left.

若人求佛，是人失佛；若人求祖，是人失祖。最珍贵之宝在你身中，是你自己，向外追求，便会失去了它。
By seeking the Buddha, we lose the Buddha; in seeking Bodhidharma, we lose Bodhidharma. The most precious thing there is resides inside you—it is your self. In pursuing external objects, we lose the self.

5

82

俱胝
一指禅
Juzhi's
One
Finger
Zen

1 俱胝刚出家不久，一个人住在草庵里自我修行。
Not long after Juzhi had become a monk, he moved into a grass hut and spent his time in solitary selfcultivation.

2 有一天，一位法号实际的女尼来到庵里，绕着俱胝走了三圈……
One day, a nun named Shiji approached his hut, walked three circles around Juzhi, and said...

3 你说得出一句，我就摘下斗笠。
If you can say just one word, I'll take off my hat you.

4 这其中含有无比的禅机，但到底是什么呢？
Oh, I know this is some kind of crafty Zen challenge, but what does it mean?!

5 既然回答不出来，我便告辞了。
Since you cannot answer, I'll take leave now.

6 她到底要我说些什么呢？她的斗笠又代表什么？
Ohh! Just what did she mean?! And what did that straw hat represent?!

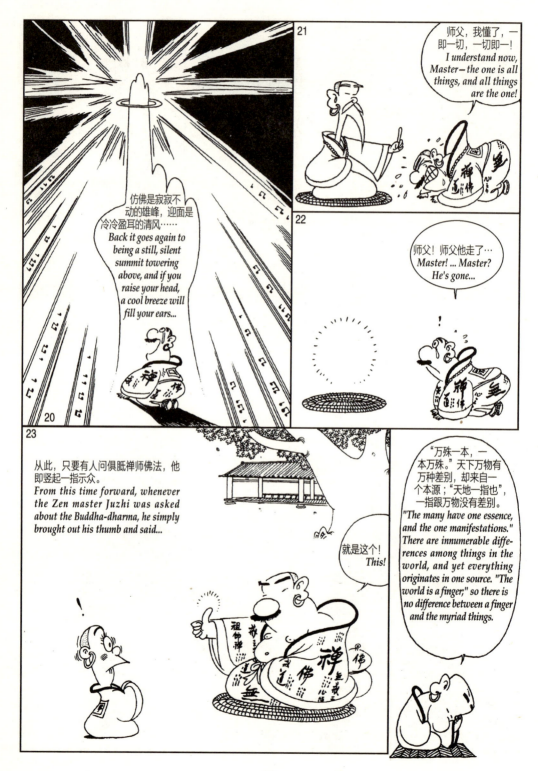

21

师父，我懂了，一即一切，一切即一—!
I understand now, Master— the one is all things, and all things are the one!

仿佛是寂寂不动的雄峰，迎面是冷冷盈耳的清风……
Back it goes again to being a still, silent summit towering above, and if you raise your head, a cool breeze will fill your ears...

20

22

师父！师父他走了…
Master! ... Master? He's gone...

23

从此，只要有人问俱胝禅师佛法，他即竖起一指示众。
From this time forward, whenever the Zen master Juzhi was asked about the Buddha-dharma, he simply brought out his thumb and said...

就是这个！
This!

"万殊一本，一本万殊。"天下万物有万种差别，却来自一个本源；"天地一指也"，一指跟万物没有差别。
"The many have one essence, and the one manifestations." There are innumerable differences among things in the world, and yet everything originates in one source. "The world is a finger," so there is no difference between a finger and the myriad things.

俱胝断指
Juzhi severs a Finger

就是这个!
This!

后来，俱胝收了一个沙弥，经常在旁边看师父以指示众……
Later, Juzhi accepted a very young monk as his disciple, and this child would sit by quietly and watch Juzhi enlighten people with his finger...

就是这个!
This!

每当俱胝不在，他就竖起一指，代替师父回答问题。
And when Juzhi wasn't around, the child would surreptitiously take his place, and in like manner, use his finger to enlighten others.

师父，有人前来参拜问法，我就代你竖指回答了!
Master, people have come to ask about the dharma, and just like you, I raise my finger in response!

这是鹦鹉学舌，算什么禅?
You might as well be a parrot. This is not Zen!

哇哇哇!
Waaaaa!

童子! 什么是佛法?
Hey kid, what is the Buddha-dharma?

师徒两人各伸出一指，沙弥看到自己断指，刹那间，顿然开悟!
The master and student both brought forth their fingers, and at the moment the young monk saw his severed finger, he was suddenly enlightened!

别人悟通体会的事理永远不可能变成自己的，除非你能从中自己悟通才能纳为己用。
What other people have come to understand intuitively can never become yours unless you come to understand it through your own efforts.

六根合一
Six in One

仰山问洪恩禅师说：
Yangshan once asked the Zen master Hongen:

如何才能得到见性的经验？
How can I have the experience of seeing my own nature?

好比有一屋子，有六道窗口，里面有一只弥猴……
It's like a small house with six open windows and a baby monkey inside...

东边有人叫一声山山，
If a person calls the monkey from the east side,

山山！
Here, Clyde!

山山答，六个窗子同时传出应唤声。
When the monkey responds, the sound will come from all six windows.

经由眼、耳、鼻、舌、身、意，这六种感官所经验到的世界是真世界吗？打破感官的局限性，用眼去听、用耳去看，你会豁然顿知。
We have six senses: seeing, hearing, smelling, tasting, feeling, and thinking. But is the world that they sense the real world? If we can overcome the inherent limitations of our senses, using our eyes to hear and our ears to see, then suddenly everything will become clear, and we will understand.

93

弥须纳芥
A Mountain in a Mustard Seed

唐朝的李勃很爱读书，由于读书破万卷，世人称他为"李万卷"。

During the Tang dynasty, there was a man named Li Bo who just loved to study. Because he had read over ten thousand volumes, people called him Li of Ten Thousand Volumes.

佛典《维摩经》中写道"须弥山没入芥子"，请问这么大的山河如何装入小小的一粒芥子之中？

There is a passage in the Vimalakirti-nirdesa which says: "Mount Sumeru can be inserted into a mustard seed." How could such a big mountain possibly fit into a tiny mustard seed?

有一次，他问智常和尚说：

One day, he asked the monk Zhishang:

啊……
Oh...

人称你是李万卷，请问你万卷书如何装入你这小小的脑袋瓜里？

You're called Li of Ten Thousand Volumes, how could those ten thousand volumes fit into your tiny skull?

"道"是无量、无边、无所不在的，它存在于芥子中。

The Dao is immeasurable, boundless, and ubiquitous. And it does exist in a tiny mustard seed.

97

木樨香自香
The Sweet Smell of Osmanthus

1. 禅宗的究竟奥义是什么?
What, after all, is the profound meaning of Zen?

2. 论语上说:"吾无隐乎尔。"禅对你也没有什么隐藏。
Confucius said: "I conceal nothing from you." Zen doesn't hide anything from you, either.

3. 我还是不懂。
I still don't get it.

4. 跟我到后山走走……
Come with me to the back side of this mountain...

5. 你有没有闻到木樨香?
Can you smell the sweet osmanthus?

那么,我也没有隐瞒你什么。
See, I'm not hiding anything from you, either.

把握现在,体悟当前,别错过人生中的每一事、每一物,夜夜是春宵,日日是好日。
Seize the moment; experience the present; don't let anything slip by. Every evening is a spring evening, and every day is a good day.

6.

101

空手而回
Returning Empty-handed

1　石头希迁本是六祖慧能的弟子，六祖入灭后他就去投奔青原行思……
The monk Shitou Xiquan was a disciple of the sixth Zen patriarch Huineng. After Huineng entered Nirvana, Shitou Xiquan went on a journey...

从曹溪六祖处来。
I'm coming from Caoxi, the place of the sixth patriarch.

你从哪里来？
Where are you from?

2　3　你从曹溪得到了什么？
And what did you gain at Caoxi?

我去曹溪之前就没缺少什么。
I didn't lack anything before I went to Caoxi.

要是我不去曹溪，又怎会知道我没缺少什么呢？
If I wouldn't have gone to Caoxi, how would I have known that I never lacked anything?

没有一位老师能把任何东西灌输给学生，但他却能帮助学生看清内心的一切。
No teacher can instil a student with anything; but he can help that student understand everything in the student's own mind.

4　那么你又何必去曹溪呢？
Then why did you go?

5　6

随流去
Follow
the Flow

1
大梅和尚悟道后，便在山中结庵隐居。
After the monk Damei had attained enlightenment, he went to live by himself in the mountains.

2
有一次，一位云水僧迷路，正好遇到他。
One day, a wandering monk became lost and happened upon Damei.

3
你在山中住了多少岁月？
How long have you lived here in the mountains?

我只看到四面八方的山变绿变黄而已。
I have only seen the surrounding mountains turn green and yellow.

4
从哪条路可以走出这山区？
Can you tell me how to get out of these mountains?

5
随流去！
Follow the flow.

行为原本很容易，但被世上的许多方圆规矩框住了，结果就变得寸步难行了。
Movement was originally easy, but we have been shackled by so many worldly rules and restrictions that it is sometimes difficult to take even a single step.

进退两难
Difficult to Advance or Retreat

法云禅师有一次对僧徒说：
The Zen master Fayun once said to his disciples:

假如你进一步，失道；退一步，失物，不进不退则像一块石头般的无知，这时要怎么办？

Suppose you were in a situation where if you were to move forward, you would lose the Dao, if you were to move backward, you would lose the world, and if you were to do neither, you would look ignorant as a stone. What would you do?

1

如何才不至于无知？
Is there any way we can get away from looking ignorant?

2

3

舍偏除执，尽你的可能去做。
Abandon both rejection and attachment and act out your potential.

4

如何才能不失道，又不离物？
But if we act, how can we keep from losing the Dao and the world?

进一步，同时又退一步。
Move forward and backward at the same time.

5

进即退，退即进，双即又双离，以达到绝对圆融的境界。

Advancing is retreating, and retreating is advancing; they both arrive and they both depart. By doing both at the same time, we can get to the realm of perfect harmony among all differences.

111

9

守端不明白老师为何而笑，整夜失眠。
Shouduan couldn't understand what his teacher found so funny and lost sleep over it all night.

8

第二天一早……
Early the next morning...

老师为何听了郁和尚的偈子而发笑？
Why did you laugh so hard at Monk Yu's poem?

10

昨天你看到那打耍的小丑没？
Did you see that silly clown that came by yesterday?

看到。
Yes.

11

你在某一方面不如那个小丑。
There is one aspect in which you are inferior to that clown.

老师指的是什么？
And what is that, Master?

12

小丑喜欢别人笑，而你却怕别人笑。
At this, Shouduan attained enlightenment.

守端听了，因而大悟。
That clown likes people to laugh, but you are afraid when people laugh.

13

禅超越了理性和反理性，求道切忌拘泥不化，把普通人之常情，看得过于严肃，过于玄妙。
Zen transcends the rational and the irrational. When seeking the Dao, be sure to avoid getting too stuffy and taking what are other people's natural reactions too seriously or too profoundly.

**丹霞烧佛
Danxia
Burns the
Buddha**

丹霞禅师有一次住宿于慧林寺，因为天气很冷而把寺内的佛像拿来烧火取暖……
Once while the Zen master Danxia was staying at Huilin Temple, the weather was bitter cold, so to keep warm, He burned a statue of the Buddha...

你真大胆，竟敢烧佛像！
You cretin! How could you burn a statue of the Buddha?!

我想看看佛像能不能烧出舍利子……
I wanted to see if any sarira, would come out...

哦？
Huh?

木佛怎能烧出舍利子？
Why would there sarira in a wooden statue?

既然不能烧出舍利子，那么这两尊也拿来烧吧！
Well if there aren't any sarira, bring them all down here to burn!

道人无心，何过之有？不拘泥于形式，率真地依本性去做，即无过错。
A man of the Dao is of nomind; how can he do wrong? By not getting mired in appearances and by following our oritinal nature, we can do no wrong.

113

心境一如
Mind Like
the
Surround-
ings

请问应该如何转山河大地归自己?
How can I get the mountains, the rivers, and the great earth to return to me?

应该要转自己归山河大地!
You should return yourself to the mountains, the rivers, and the great earth!

若想以"我"吸取真理,则尚未全然抛弃"我",这样便无法得到完全的真理。应该使自己和世界同化,诚心地忘我才能与真理结合为一。
If you try to attract the truth through the self, then you've yet to completely abandon the self, and you'll never get to the complete truth. Only by assimilating yourself with nature and sincerely forgetting the self can you be one with the truth.

什么不是佛法?
What Isn't the Byddha-dharma

有一侍僧向鸟窠和尚辞行……
As a disciple was taking leave of the monk Niaowo...

你到哪里去？
Where are you off to?

多谢您的教诲，我要走了。
Thank you very much for everything. I'll be going now.

云游天下学习佛法。
I'm going to travel the land studying the Buddha-dharma.

说到佛法，我这里也有一点……
Speaking of the Buddha-dharma, I have a bit of it right here...

在哪里？
Where?

于是鸟窠就抽出一根布毛……
At this, Niaowo pulled a thread from his sleeve...

这不也是佛法吗？
Is this not the Buddha-dharma, as well?

万物的原理并不在远不可及的地方，它就在我们心中。万物皆有佛性，什么不是佛法？只要你能去体会"它"。
The truth of things does not reside in some unreachable distant place; it is in our minds. Everything possesses the Buddha-nature, so what is there that isn't the Buddha-dharma? You just have to try to understand it intuitively.

抓住虚空
Grasping
Emptiness

你能不能抓住虚空？
Can you grab ahold of emptiness?

能。
Sure.

石巩问师弟西堂智藏说：
Shigong asked a youngfer master, Xitang Zhicang :

1

那么你抓抓看。
Well, Let's see you do it.

好。
Ok.

2

3

4

只是这样吗? 结果你并没有抓住什么呀!
Is that it? You didn't get anything!

那么你认为应该怎么抓?
Then how would you do it?

5

应该像这样抓!
Ow! That hurts! That hurts?

哇! 痛痛痛痛痛。
Like this!

既然色（物质）即是空，空即是色，那么与其伸手去扑个空，倒不如捏住对方的鼻子来得更能接近真实。
Since matter is empty, and emptiness is matter, grabbing a piece of emptiness isn't as close to reality as just reaching out and grabbing the other person's nose is.

6

118

眼前问
即是道路
The Road
Begins Here

十方都通佛土，一条大路直通
涅槃之门，请问路由哪里走起？
*All directions lead to the land of
the Buddha, and one road leads
directly to the gates of Nirvana.
Please tell me where this
road begins.*

学僧问乾峰禅师说：
*A student asked the Zen
master Qianfeng:*

1

就从这里。
Right here.

人生的道理不需要往虚
无缥缈的世界去寻找，只要
注意生活的细节，从生活上去
体认即可。当人的怀疑刚刚兴起，
答案可能就摆在那里。
*You don't need to travel to some
illusory world to find the principles of life; just pay attention to
the details of life and experience
them. When you begin to doubt,
an answer is most likely found
where the question begins.*

2

123

麻三斤
Three Pounds of Flax

什么是佛？
What is the Buddha?

云游僧问洞山守初和尚说：
The monk Yunyou once asked the monk Shouchu of Dongshan:

麻三斤。
Three pounds of flax.

我请洞山和尚解释佛的意义，他却回答"麻三斤"，这是什么意思？
I asked Dongshan what the Buddha is, and he answered, "Three pounds of flax." What did he mean?

该僧转问智门和尚道：
Yunyou then went to ask the monk Zhimen:

有如群花盛开编锦织。
Like a meadow of flowers woven into a silk brocade.

还是不懂……
I still don't get it...

南地之竹，北地之木。
Southern bamboo and northern trees.

越听越不懂……
The more I listen, the less I understand...

6

云游僧只好又回来请教洞山和尚。
Yunyou revint vers le moine Dongshan. Il le questionna à nouveau.

7

言语只是表达事实的工具，凡执着于言辞即会丧失真实，更会迷乱不止。
Language is merely a tool for expressing facts. Whoever insists o language sacrifices the truth and will be coufused forever.

如以石掷狗时，狗会追石子；但以石掷狮子时，狮子却不理采石块而会直扑投掷的人身。故不可像狗而要学狮子来探讨禅语。
For instance, if a rock is thrown at a dog, the dog will go after the rock; but if a rock is thrown at a lion, the lion will go after the person who threw it. When investigating the language of Zen, you should be like the lion and not the dog.

8

9

禅者的言辞只是"境界语"，是一种"话头"带引你进入更深一层的境涯，故不能光是追逐禅语本身的字意。
The words of a person of Zen are just pointers, topics that lead to a deeper level of experience, so when encountering the language of Zen, don't pursue simply the meanings of the words themselves.

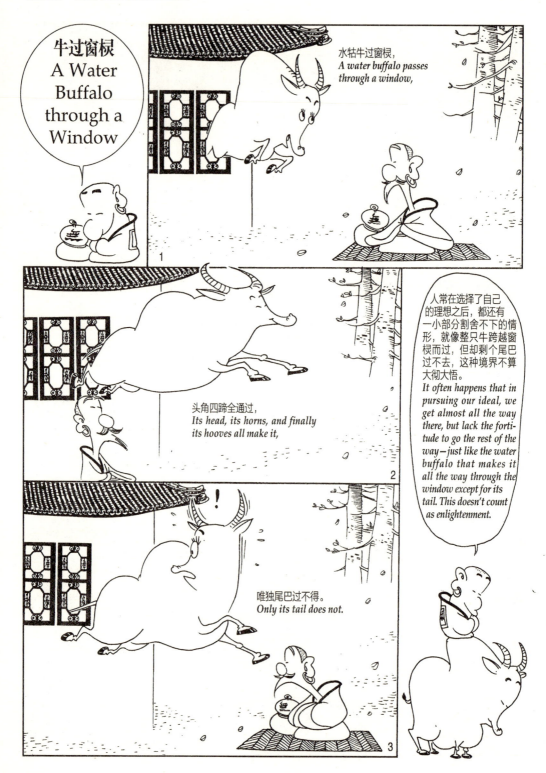

牛过窗棂
A Water
Buffalo
through a
Window

水牯牛过窗棂，
A water buffalo passes through a window,

人常在选择了自己的理想之后，都还有一小部分割舍不下的情形，就像整只牛跨越窗棂而过，但却剩个尾巴过不去，这种境界不算大彻大悟。
It often happens that in pursuing our ideal, we get almost all the way there, but lack the fortitude to go the rest of the way—just like the water buffalo that makes it all the way through the window except for its tail. This doesn't count as enlightenment.

头角四蹄全通过，
Its head, its horns, and finally its hooves all make it,

唯独尾巴过不得。
Only its tail does not.

126

做自己的
主人公
Being
Your
Own
Master

1
有物先天地，
There was something
before heaven
and earth,

2
无形本寂寥。
it was formless and originally quiescent.

能为万物主，
It had the power of mastery over all things.

不逐四时凋。
It did not wither
with the four
seasons.

人与混沌本一体，无分无别；无分别者一也，一者道也，道即佛也，禅也。能真正做自己的主人，就不再会因环境、对象的不同，而改变自己。
Originally we were all a part of primal chaos, inseparable, indistinguishable. The inseparable is one; the one is Dao; the Dao is the Buddha, Zen. He who is the master of himself does not change through influence fron his surroundings or form others.

3
4

127

一朝风月
A Morning
of the Moon
and Wind

善能是南宋的一位禅师，他常说：
Shanneng was a Zen master during the Southern Song dynasty who often said:

不可以一朝风月，
Do not let one day's clear moon,

1　2

而昧却万古常空；
Obscure the eternal emptiness of the interminable past;

3

不可以万古常空，
Do not let the eternal emptiness of theinterminable past,

而不明一朝风月。
Obscure one day's clear moon.

4　5

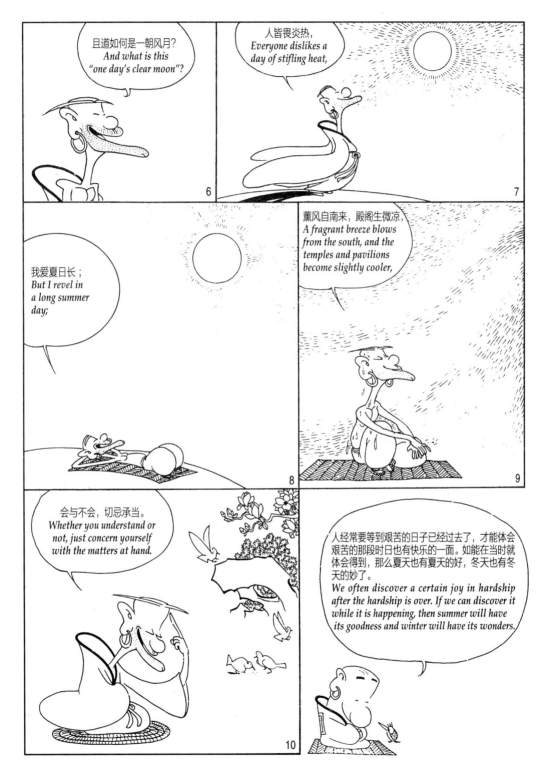

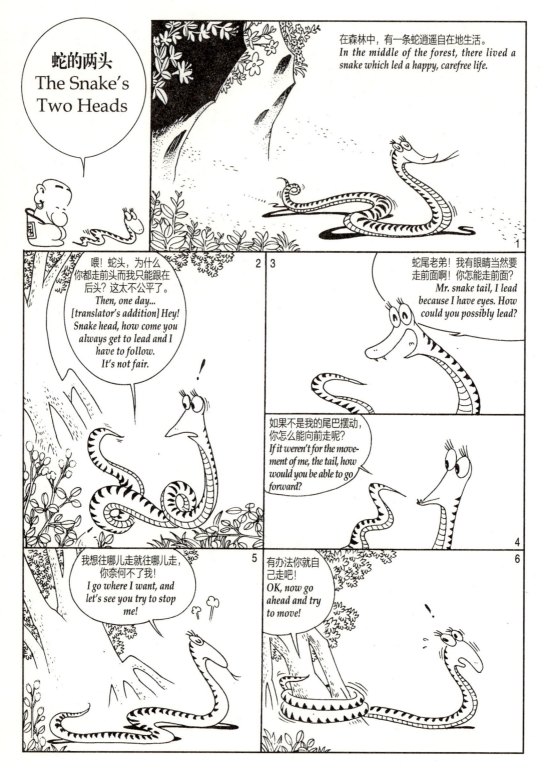

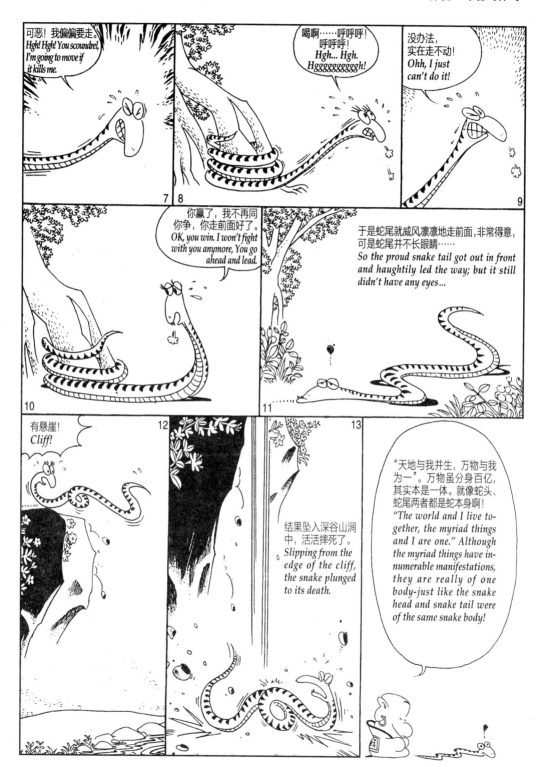

蜘蛛之丝
The Spider's Silk

释尊有一次坐在花园的井边，探头往井里望去……
One day while Sakyamuni was sitting in a garden by the side of a well, his eyes were drawn deep down into the well...

1

！

哇哇哇哇哇！
Ahhhhhhhh-hh!

哇哇哇哇哇！
Ahhhhhhhh-hh!

2

救救我……我好苦哦，救救我啊……
Help! Help me! I'm suffering terribly! Ohh!...

3

这个人生前作恶多端，死后才会在地狱受苦啊……
This man must have been very evil during his lifetime to suffer like this in Hell...!

4

5

他一生中干的都是杀人放火无恶不作的勾当，难道都不曾做过任何一件善事吗？
All he did throughout his life was kill and pillage with reckless abandon, and there was no act too evil for him. But didn't he do at lease one good thing?

6

啊……有了！有一次走路正要踩到一只小蜘蛛时，他突生恻隐之心，没有将蜘蛛踩死，虽然这只是件小事，但毕竟还算是善业啊……
Ah, yes! Once when he was about to step on a spider, he had a moment of compassion and spared its life. Of course it's just a small matter, but it is good...

7

好吧，就用这只小蜘蛛的力量，将他救离苦海吧……
OK. then, we'll let this spider save him from his pit of suffering...

8

9

10

啊……一条蜘蛛丝从天上垂下来。
Eh? A string of spider's silk descends from above.

135

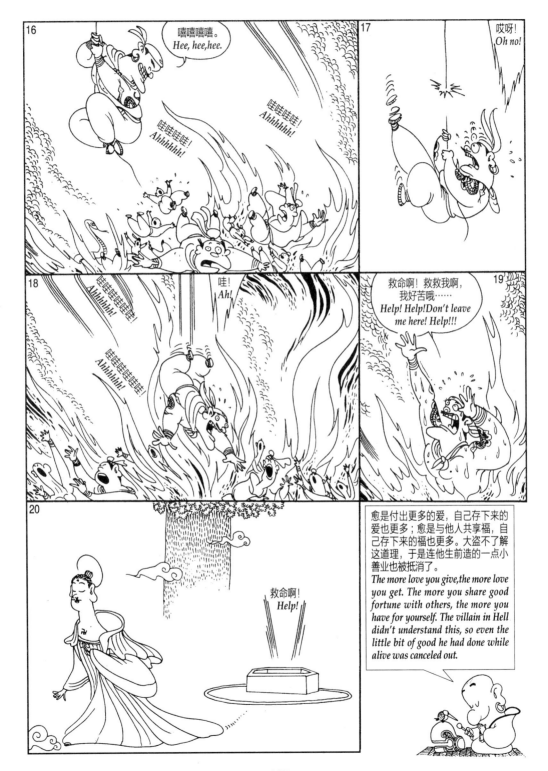

137

141

附录 · 延伸阅读
APPENDIX Further reading

此部分为本书图画页的延伸阅读，各段首所示的页码与图画页对应。

P1—P8 达摩大师说："不立文字，教外别传，直指人心，见性成佛"是指出禅的立宗的基础及体验的方法。既是"教外别传"，故无所依之经典；既"不立文字"，故亦无由以见理论的构想；只以"见性"一事，为"成佛"之道而已。所以古人说"禅宜默不宜说"；或谓"禅之一字，非圣凡所测"。

禅是一个最奇妙的东西，它不是任何事物，任何事物也都不出它的范围。它涵盖一切，同时也泯绝一切。这里所说的涵盖，并不是说它具备一切事物；这里所说的泯绝，并不是说它离开一切事物。它和一切事物的关系，是建立在不即不离上面。

现代的科学，在外形上，得区别人类与其他的存在物，可是谈到内面的存在，可说便是不能认清彼此的区别了。所以在禅观物，把万有生命的"法性"与人类的"佛性"，只就自觉的有无方面而标异其名，至于本质，便没有什么不同，故从这一元的立场成立万物一体观，是不应强划分其区别的。

南隐是日本明治时代（一八六八——一九一二）的一位禅师。有一天，有位大学教授来向他问禅，他只以茶相待。他将茶水注入这位来宾的杯中，直到杯满，而后又继续注入。

这位教授眼睁睁地望着茶水不息地溢出杯外，他再也不能沉默下去了，终于说道："已经漫出来了，不要再倒了！""你就像这只杯子一样，"南隐答道："里面装满了你自己的看法和想法。你不先把你自己的杯子空掉，叫我如何对你说禅？"

无字，是参禅的人首先应该透过的关门，是佛性开显的第一步。因有了这一步的飞跃，才得打开涅槃的妙境；可是这必须的要件，不是学说的研究，只是穷迫向自己的心路；要心路绝处，那就不可不蓦直地精进努力才得。

所以禅是把有无、凡圣、迷悟等的概念一切抛下，而入于无的三昧，使心成"无化"；一达到无的极致时，真如识自然自内发动起来，因之触着这发动的妙机。

据禅的立场说：宇宙间的东西，都是独自存在，没有对立的，一切都是超对立的存在。所以生也、死也，原是一样；既没有与生相对的死，也没有与死相对的生，这就是"生死即涅槃"的意思。

离了一切对立，即是实相的境地，在这里，开始从根本主体上出现活动，创造新生命；于是真法、真智、真性，在这里显现。

慧能大师对"禅"有如下解释："何名禅定？外离相为禅，内不乱为定。外若着相，内心即乱。本性自净自定。只为见境思境即乱。若见诸境心不乱者，是真定也。善知识！外离相即禅，内不乱即定。外禅内定，是为禅定。"慧能认为心始终不着于外相（即心不去追逐外境及内意识的事物），时时呈现出一种安详与宁静的喜悦与自由，这就是禅的最基本含义。

世尊昔在灵山会上拈花示众，众皆默然，唯迦叶尊者破颜微笑。世尊云："吾有正法眼藏，涅槃妙心，实相无相微妙法门，不立文字，教外别传，付嘱摩诃迦叶。"

无门曰：黄面瞿昙旁若无人，压良为贱，悬羊头卖狗肉，将谓多少奇特。只如当时大众都笑，正法眼藏作么生传？设使迦叶不笑，正法眼藏又作么生传？若道正法眼藏有传授，黄面老子诳谝闾阎；若道无传授，为什么独许迦叶？颂曰：拈起花来，尾巴已露。迦叶破颜，人天罔措！

《无门关》

P9 迦叶尊者，即摩诃迦叶，禅宗印度法系的第一祖。

实相本无相，可是拈起花来，已露形相，所以说已泄天机，露了尾巴。在这里便不能在拈花处大做文章，应该想想花未拈起前，是什么样的境界。

迦叶这一破颜而笑，使得所有的天、人都懵然不知。因为迦叶何所见而笑，只有迦叶自己知道。这只许自知，乃是正法眼藏，涅槃妙心，不是文字语言所能表达的。不过迦叶的这一笑，也已有了相，如果后人都学迦叶的破颜，禅宗岂不变成了一场闹剧？

吴怡《公案禅语》

P10—P11 在佛学经典中，对于破时破空的文字特别多。如《华严经》云："以一劫为一切劫，以一切劫为一劫（时）。以一切刹为一刹，以一刹为一切刹（空）。"《维摩诘经》云："以四大海水入一毛孔，断取三千大千世界，如陶家轮，着右掌中（空）。演七日以为一劫，促一劫以为七日（时）。"都是一方面破时，一方面破空。

迦叶因阿难问："世尊传金襕袈裟外，别传何物？"叶唤云："阿难！"难应："诺！"叶云："倒却门前刹竿着！"

无门曰：若向者里下得一转语亲切，便见灵山一会俨然未散。其或未然：毗婆尸佛早留心，直至而今不得妙！颂曰：问处何如答处亲？几人于此眼生筋？兄呼弟应扬家丑，不属阴阳别是春！

《无门关》

P12—P16 某次，坦山与一道友走上一条泥浆路，此时，天上仍在下着大雨。他俩在一个拐弯处遇到一位漂亮的女郎，因为身着绸布衣裳和丝质的衣带而无法跨过那条泥路。

"来吧，姑娘。"坦山说道，然后就把那位女郎抱过了泥路。

道友一直闷声不响，直到天黑挂单寄宿，才按捺不住地对坦山说："我们出家人不近女色，特别是年轻貌美的女子，那是很危险的。你为什么要那样做？"

"什么？那个女人吗？"坦山答道，"我早就把她放下了，你还抱着吗？"

众生自无始以来，生活方式与生活环境，各有不同，故习染亦有差异。因此对于同一事物，各有不同的观点。但其动机则一，那就是我执观念。只要是与自己利害有关的，便立即表现出来。佛家将这种本能的意识活动，称为无明。断习就是要断掉无明。鱼朝恩问慧忠国师曰："何者是无明，无明从何时起？"师曰："佛法衰相今现，奴也解问佛法。"此语对鱼朝恩当然是一种侮辱。鱼朝恩当时勃然变色。师曰："此是无明，无明从此起。"鱼朝恩当即有省。

大愚和愚堂两位禅师，奉邀去见一位大臣。刚一到达，愚堂就对这位大官说道："你天性聪敏，能够学禅。"

"胡扯，"大愚说道，"你怎么奉承这个呆头？他虽居高位，但对禅一窍不通。"

结果，这位大官没有为愚堂建庙，却给大愚造了一座，且跟他学禅。

143

在一切差别相中，只要我们有超越物我，超越自他的理念，就能证得真我。佛是干矢橛，佛是麻三斤。要从干矢橛中和麻三斤中悟得佛性。有超越感的，处处是佛。

六祖有一次向大众说："我这里有一个东西，无头无尾，无名无字，无背无面，你们是否认识呢？"神会答道："他是诸佛的本源，神会的佛性。"六祖说："我已告诉你是无名无字的，你偏要叫他作本源和佛性。将来你有一间盖头的茅屋，也只是一个知解宗徒。"自性一落知解，便变成识心中的事物。宗门禅的特点，是"教外别传，不立文字"。所以有了知解，便与不立文字的宗旨不符。向居士云："无名作名，因其名则是非生矣。无理作理，因其理则争论起矣。"

周中一《禅话》

P17—P25 禅家是以真我为主体，真我是不受躯壳的限制的。但人情上总觉得死是永恒的离开尘世，免不了悲哀。感情脆弱的人，往往承受不了这种悲哀的打击。六祖临终时，徒众痛哭。他告诉大家："我是另有去处，你们不必悲哀。"六祖是把生死一样的看待，死不过是等于旅行途中换一个旅舍而已。自己既知道了去处，自可处之泰然。

在日本，禅宗尚未传入之前，天台宗的学者即已坐禅。那时有同学四人，非常要好，但为了避免闲扯打岔而好好用功打坐起见，他们约定：誓守不语戒七天。头一天的白天，他们都静默不语，故而打坐的效果也非常之好。但到了夜深之际，油灯忽明忽暗，眼看就要熄了。他们中的一位禁不住向侍从叫道："请添些灯油！"另一位同学听了颇以为怪。"我们应该一言不发的呀！"他说。

"你俩真蠢，"另一位同学说道，"为什么偏要讲话呢？"

"只有我没有讲话！"第四位同学应道。

山冈铁舟到处参访名师。一天，他见了相国寺的独园和尚。为了表示他的悟境，他颇为得意地对独园说道："心、佛、以及众生，三者皆空。现象的真性是空。无悟、无迷、无圣、无凡、无施、无受。"

当时独园正在抽烟，未曾答腔。但他突然举起烟管将山冈打了一下，使得这位年轻的禅者至为愤怒。

"一切皆空，"独园问道，"哪儿来这么大的脾气？"

杨黼离别双亲到四川去拜访无际菩萨，在路上碰到了一个老和尚，那和尚问他："你去哪里"？杨黼告诉对方他要去做无际的学生，老和尚便说："与其去找菩萨，还不如去找佛。"杨黼问："哪里有佛啊？"老和尚回答："你回家时，看到有个人披着毯子，穿反了鞋来迎接你，记住，那就是佛。"

杨黼依照吩咐回家，在抵家的那天，已是深夜，他的母亲已睡觉了，一听到儿子叫门，高兴得来不及穿衣，便披上毯子当外衣，匆忙中，拖鞋也穿错了脚，赶紧来迎接儿子，杨黼一看到母亲这种情形，立刻大悟，此后他便专心侍奉双亲，并写了一大部的孝经注。

师自黄梅得法，回至韶州曹侯村，人无知者，时有儒士刘志略，礼遇甚厚。志略有姑为尼，名"无尽藏，"常诵《大涅槃经》。师暂听，即知妙义，遂为解说。尼乃执卷问字。师曰："字即不识，义即请问。"尼曰："字尚不识，焉能会义。"师曰："诸佛妙理，非关文字。"尼惊异之。遍告里中耆德云："此是有道之士，宜请供养。"有魏武侯玄孙曹叔良及居民，竞来瞻礼。

达摩祖师的行入门有四种，第一是："报怨行"：凡今生所遭受的一切痛苦，都是过去生中所造的业。不必怨天尤人。菩萨畏因不畏果；一切听凭业力的牵引，随遇而安，便不为道障。

一天晚上，七里禅师正在诵经之时，一名强盗带着一把尖刀进来向他表示：要不拿钱出来，就要他的老命。七里对他说道："不要打扰我。钱在那个抽屉里，你自己去拿。"说罢继续诵经。

这个闯入者拿了他大部分的钱，正要走开。"收人家礼物应该说声谢谢。"七里说道。那人向他致谢后立即走了。数天之后，这个强盗被捕了，他招认抢窃多处，受害人中包含有七里在内。当七里被召作证时，他说："此人不是强盗，至少，据我所知确是如此。钱是我给他的，他已谢过我了。"

此人服刑期满后即来叩见七里，求他收为徒弟。

自性是不分时间与空间而充塞宇宙的。我们无法用六根去接触到他。语言是由意根与舌根所产生的；代表语言的文字，也是在意根指挥之下，用手描画出来的。都是只能表诠现象界的事物，不能表诠超越现象的自性。

慧林慈受有如下面一段对话：

和尚问："当一个人感觉到而说不出，他像什么？"慈受说："他像哑巴吃蜜。"和尚问："当一个人并没有感觉到，却谈得有声有色，他像什么？"慈受说："他像鹦鹉叫人。"

禅宗要我们学习哑巴，无论是苦、是甜，或是梦，都不足与外人道。最犯忌的就是像鹦鹉一样，心中毫无所得，只在嘴巴上乱说，而流于文字禅、口头禅。

吴经熊著　吴怡译《禅学的黄金时代》

P26—P31 一休禅师自幼就很聪明。他的老师有一只非常珍爱的茶杯，是件稀世之宝。一天，他无意中将它打破了，内心感到非常狼狈。但就在这时候，他听到了老师的脚步声，连忙把打破的茶杯藏在背后。当他的老师走到他面前时，他忽然开口问道："人为什么一定要死呢？"

"这是自然之事，"他的老师答道，"世间的一切，有生就有死。"

这时，一休拿出打破的茶杯接着说道："你的茶杯死期到了！"

契冲是明治时代的大师之一，曾任京都大教堂东福寺的住持多年。一天，京都总督首次造访，他的侍者将有"京都总督北垣"字样的名片送到他的面前。

"我与这个家伙没有瓜葛，"契冲对他的侍者说道，"叫他出去！"侍者送回名片，表示歉意。"那是我的错误，"总督说道，用笔将"京都总督"四字涂掉，"烦请再问你的老师。"

"噢，是北垣啊！"这位大师看了名片说道，"我要见见这个家伙！"

佛教旨在为人解决痛苦，释尊因而离家。人常以自我为中心去看事物，若事与愿违，则难免心生苦痛。

事物乃由缘起、变化、空、无我、不污染等要素构成。但是，自己被污染、固执、反抗命运、与人争夺、好与人比较等，或只站在自私的立场去衡量他人，皆是痛苦的元凶。

会对不污染的事实（真理）产生共鸣，就能舍去自我为主的观念，以无我去面对他人，如此使自己配合真理并为之同化，这才是佛教的目的。

别把它当成知识或理论，只当是自己的心态，而将自己融入事实（真实），这需要有心之突破的体验才行。

但人们对自己的身体、心、习惯、经验等，都有既成的想法，几乎不能用无我的眼光，去看事物的真相，即使自以为很认真地看，事实上却看不见。甚至根本没有站在事物的立场去思考的经验，此乃尚未脱离躯壳的缘故。

生死也是一种时空形式，生时必定占有一个空间；死后躯壳不存在了，就失去以前所占有的空间。由生到死的一段距离，便是时间。最足以说明无常的生灭法的，莫过于生死了。谁都希望自己的空间占得很大，时间占得很长。由这种时空观念，又产生了我、人、众、寿的四相，乃至一切对待观念。所以生死观念，是一切时空观念中最重要的一环，也是人们意识中最难处理和最难遣除的问题。

问："学人乍入丛林，乞师指个入路。"师（玄沙）曰："还闻偃溪水声否？"曰："闻。"师曰："是汝入处。"

《景德传灯录》

P32-P36 有一位名叫信长的日本伟大武士,有一次他决心要打实力比他强上十倍的敌人。他很有信心打胜这场硬仗,但他的部下则颇为怀疑。

在他带队前进的途中,他在一座神社的前面停下,对他的部下说道:"我要在参拜这座神社之后投钱问卜。如果正面朝上,表示我们会赢,否则则输。我们的命运操在神的手里。"

信长进入神社,默默祷告了一会儿。然后转身,当众投下一枚硬币。结果正面朝上。于是他的部下都急着要去攻打敌人,恨不得马上就打赢这场硬仗。

"谁也不能改变命运的掌握。"打胜之后,他的一位随从说道。

"诚然如此,"信长说道,说着抖出一枚硬币,两面都是正面。

柳生又寿郎是一位著名的剑手之子。他的父亲认为他学习成绩太差,不能精通剑道而与他脱离父子关系。于是他前往二荒山去见名剑手武藏,武藏也肯定了他父亲的判断。"你要跟我学剑吗?"武藏问道,"你不能满足我的要求的。"

"但是,假如我努力学习的话,需要多少年才能成为一名剑师?"这位青年坚持着问道……

大道即是"只要无憎爱,即可洞然明白"。所谓的洞然又是什么呢?洞然就是没有障碍。若细观日常生活,则到处都充满障碍。障与碍是同样的东西,都是碍手碍脚的意思。但为何又会导致碍手碍脚呢?这是由于自己有喜好与厌恶的缘故。

耽源禅师将忠国师所传之九十六圆相给仰山,仰山一览便烧却。隔日师谓仰山曰:"九十六圆相,乃是忠国师从上祖传下来的,你须善为保存。"仰山曰:"我已焚之。"师问:"何故焚之?"曰:"用得便可,不可拘执。若必要者,可重绘之。"次日,耽源上堂验仰山。仰山作呈相式,叉手而立。耽源两手交作拳式示之。仰山进前作女式礼拜。耽遂肯之。

周中一《禅话》

P37 伯牙鼓琴,钟子期听之,方鼓琴,而志在太山,钟子期曰:"善哉乎鼓琴,巍巍乎若太山。"少选之间,而志在流水,钟子期又曰:"善哉乎鼓琴,汤汤乎若流水。"钟子期死,伯牙破琴绝弦,终身不复鼓琴,以为世无足复为鼓琴者。

《吕氏春秋》

P38-P45 一位盲人拜访了朋友,辞去时,因天色已黑,朋友就给他一只灯笼,让他照路回家。"我不需要灯笼,"他说,"无论明暗,对我都是一样。"

"我知道你不需要灯笼,"朋友说道,"但你如果不带的话,别人也许会撞着你。"

这位盲者带着灯笼走了,但走不多远,却被有人撞个正着。"看你走到哪里去了!"他对来人叫道,"难道你看不见这盏灯笼?""老兄,你的蜡烛已经熄了。"那人说道。

良宽禅师居住在山脚下的一座小茅棚中,生活过得非常简单。一天晚上,小偷光顾他的茅庐,结果发现没有一样东西值得一偷。

良宽从外面回来,碰见了这位老兄。"你也许是跋涉长途而来,"他对小偷说道,"不该空手而回。请把我身上的衣服当作礼物拿去吧。"小偷感到不知所云,拿了衣服就溜。

良宽赤着身子坐下看月。"可怜的家伙,"他在心里沉吟道,"可惜我不能把这美丽的月亮也送给他!"

仪山禅师,一日洗澡,因水太热,叫他的一个年轻弟子提桶冷水,冲凉一些。这位弟子奉命提了水来,将热水冲凉了,便把剩下的水倾在地上。

"笨蛋!"仪山骂道,"大小事物各有用处,何不活用?给树树也欢喜,水也活着。何不拿去浇浇花草？你凭什么要浪费寺里的一滴水？"

听到这里，这位年轻的弟子竟然因此开悟了，于是将他的法号改为"滴水"，终于成了受人尊重的"滴水和尚"。

当我们生理上失去平衡时，就有了痛、痒、劳、逸种种不同的感觉。得到平衡时，便失去一切感觉。心理上失去平衡时，便有喜、怒、哀、乐、善、恶、是、非的观念。所谓动念即乖。一得到平衡，便一切都寂静了。庄子所谓："鱼相忘乎江湖，人相忘乎道术。"便是一种平衡的境界。

佛陀在一部经中说了如下一则寓言：一个人在荒野经过，碰到了一只老虎，于是他拼命逃跑，但那老虎却紧追不舍。他跑到一处悬崖之上，以两手攀着一根野藤，让全身悬在半空中摇荡。他抬头仰望，只见那只老虎向他怒吼，向下看去，又见远远的下方有另一只老虎张着血盆大口在等着他。这使他胆战心惊，颤抖不已，而他只有一条枯藤可以维系。

就在此时，又有一只白鼠和一只黑鼠，正一点一点地啃噬那条枯藤。但他忽见附近有粒鲜美的草莓，于是他以一手攀藤，以另一手去采草莓，将它送入口中，尝了一下：味道好美呀！

"无我"是佛家的一句很普遍的口号，而这一句口号，也只有佛家才有。不仅是人与人之间，无自他的分别；乃至物我的分别，也一概扫除。换言之：就是无主体、客体之分。表达此一意义的，佛家有一个很特殊而又最是恰当的名相：就是"能所两忘"，或者是称"能所一如"。能是指能够自主的我，所是指我所接触的一切事物，也就是我以外一切的环境。凡是被六根所能接触到的一切事物都是所。简言之：能所便是主体和客体。"能所两忘"，或"能所一如"的意义，便是没有自他的分别，没有物我的分别。一切事，一切处，一切时，一切物，都没有我；也可以说是一切都是我。只要没有分别，没有对待。说是无我也可以，说是唯我也可以。任何事物，都融化在自我一体以内；而自我也融化在一切事物以内。是绝对待的自我，而非有对待的自我。这个景象，便是中庸所说的"合内外之道"；孟子所说的"上下与天地同流"；老子所说的"玄同"；庄子所说的"天地与我并生，万物与我为一"；王阳明所说的"天人合一"。黄檗禅师云："心若平等，不分高下，即与众生诸佛，世界山河，有相无相，偏十方界，一切平等，无彼我相。此本源清净心，常自圆满，光明遍照也。"到达能所一如的境界，只有证悟者才能够有此胸襟。所以僧肇云："会万物为自己者，其唯圣人乎。"石头读到这两句时叹赏不已。自己又写下几句，以广其意："圣人无己，靡所不已，法身无象，谁云自他。圆鉴灵照于其间，万物体玄而自现。境智非二，孰云去来，至哉斯语也。"佛家特别强调我空、法空，我空之中就无自他的分别；法空之中就无物我的分别。自他、物我的分别都无，即是超越主客。

周中一《禅话》

P46—P47 有僧问："要如何披露自己，才能与道相合？"法眼说："你何时披露了自己，而与道不相合？"问的人是以为有道的人，另有一种与众不同的做法。法眼的答复，是认为一切皆是道，并不是在你的日常生活以外，另有一个与道相合的做法。

镰仓寿福寺的益中和尚是绘画名家，有一天，延光入道到寺拜访，取出一轴，上书"直指人心，见性成佛"八字，要和尚画出这种境界之下的"心"。和尚立刻拿起笔来，往他脸上一点，入道非常生气，和尚就把那副生气的脸孔画了出来。入道再要求画"见性成佛"的"性"，和尚却拿着笔不画，只说"画好了"。入道不了解什么意思。和尚又说："你若没有见性的眼睛就看不到"，入道是个无眼字（未能展开了悟之智眼的人），硬要和尚画"性"，和尚只好说："你先拿出性来让我瞧瞧，我就替你画。"这时入道才无言以对。

《一日一禅》引自《虚堂录》

P48-P53　纵使是对于一件不相为谋的事情，要想放开个人一己的看待方法，采取一个全新而又不同的观点，也是一种困难的事。要想搁开吾人自幼受教而得的宗教观念和信仰，更是难上加难。但是，除非你能放开你的通常观点，否则便无法了解你所关注的究系什么，以及何以和为谁。

庄子谓："至人之用心若镜，不将不迎，应物而不藏。"后天的知见、完全是经验的与料，禅师们是不需要这些知见，而是要超越一切知见的。同时禅是无任何对象可以凝思，也不是一种抽象的冥想。它要超越一切知见，才能触及人的内奥，使你得到一种真、善、美的感觉。经云："有见即为垢，此则未为见；远离于诸见，如是乃见佛。"

朱子云："动时静便在这里，动时也有静。应理而动，则虽动亦静也。事物之来，若不顺理而应，则虽块然不交于物以求静，心亦必不得静。……动静无端，亦无截然为动为静之理。"

有沙弥自幼被寺僧收养，从未见过女人。寺僧经常指着仕女画像告诉沙弥，说是吃人的老虎。沙弥年稍长，随僧至村市中一行。回寺以后，僧问沙弥云："你下山所见到的东西，你喜欢哪一样？"沙弥毫不犹疑地说："我最喜欢吃人的老虎。"食色，性也。乃无始以来的习染，断之最难。多少学道的人，断送在色字上，所以禅门中有饮酒食肉的禅师，但从不闻犯色戒而能证道者。这是禅人最紧要的一关。

后阳成天皇参于愚堂，问道："以禅而言，此心即佛，是否？"愚堂答道："倘我说是，你将以为你不会而会；倘我说不是，则我与大家所熟知的事实相违。"

另一次，天皇问愚堂："悟了的人死时向什么处去？"愚堂答道："不知。"

"为何不知？"天皇问道。

"因为我还没有死。"愚堂答道。

当此同一境性一旦达到之时，身为剑手的我，也就没有面对着我并威胁着要刺杀我的对手可见了。我似乎已使我自己变成了对手，而他所做的每一个动作和他所想的每一个念头，也就是我自己的动作和念头一样被我感到了，而我也就直觉地，甚或不知不觉地知道何时以及如何去刺他了。所有这一切，似乎均皆自然而然，毫不勉强。

高野武义《剑术心理学》

P54-P56　禅家有一句流行的口号："放下屠刀，立地成佛。"屠刀是指习染而言。只要断除习染，马上就成佛。无始以来的习心活动，想一下就停下来，这是不可能的事。所以禅家告诉人要想认识自性，必须大死一番。便是以前的我，譬如昨日死，以后的我，譬如今日生。尽管顿悟可以成佛，但在未悟以前，还是经过一番困苦来的。

五祖法演禅师云："我这里禅如人作贼，引子入人宅，教其子入柜取衣。子才入柜，爷便闭却；并于厅上扣打，惊动主人。自己先逃归。主人知有贼，点火烛之。贼子在柜中作鼠啮声。主人遣婢开柜。贼子耸身吹灭灯，推婢走出。主人及家人赶至中路，贼子忽见一井，推巨石投井中，主人于井中觅贼。而贼已逃归。其父闻知其脱险情形，说你可以做贼了。"禅是要自悟的，在自己的心中，找寻出路，别人帮不了忙的。

有人挖地挖到了一尊金罗汉，价值连城，那人却反而十分苦恼。家人问他原因，便回答说："还有其他十七尊不知埋在哪里呢！"

《不亦快哉·中国式幽默笑话》

P57-P60　日置默仙住在丹波的一座寺院里。他的一位信徒跑来向他诉苦说他的老婆太吝啬了。一天，默仙去看这位信徒的太太，在她面前握起一只拳来。"你是什么意思？"这位太太讶异地问道。"假如我的拳头永远这样，始终不变，你称那叫什么？"他问。"畸形。"这位太太答道。

接着，他又在她眼前把手伸开问道："假如这只手永远这样，始终不变，你又称它做什么？""还不是畸形？""只要你多多了解这点，"默仙说道，"你就是一位贤内助。"

自此之后，这位太太相夫教子，非常贤慧；不仅节俭，也懂施舍了。

人类生活方式愈趋复杂，所接触的事物愈多，语言文字也随着逐渐增加。众生成年累月，就被这许许多多代表事物名相的声音和符号牵着走。东西南北，上下古今，装满了一脑子的名相，替人类带来不少的烦恼，也难怪孔老先生说："我欲无言。"其实言语所能诠表的一切事物，都是虚化不实。它在自性上是浑然一体的，无任何差别之相。千变万化的波澜，只有湿性是不变的和相同的。自性亦复如是。在绝对待的自性上，一切名言都安立不上，也就无法用语言来诠表他。所以佛家把一切名言，都称为增语。假如对自性上加一句增语便是从识心上所流露出来的。禅师们在证悟以后，绝不肯用语言去诠表自性。他们教导学人，都是用旁敲侧击的方法，也不直接指出怎样是自性，同时也不许你说出自性是怎样的。释尊在灵山会上，拿着一花朵，面对大众，不发一语。这时听众们都面面相觑，不知所以。只有迦叶尊者会心地一笑。释尊便高兴地说："我有正法眼藏，涅槃妙心，实相无相，微妙法门，不立文字，教外别传，付嘱摩诃迦叶。"禅就是这样在不开口的做法中诞生的。

师一夜登山经行，忽云开见月，大笑一声，应沣阳东九十许里，居民尽谓东家。明晨递相推问，直至药山徒众云："昨夜和尚山顶大笑。"李翱再赠诗曰：选得幽居惬野情，终年无送亦无迎；有时直上孤峰顶，月下披云笑一声。

《景德传灯录》

P61–P62　其院主僧再三请和尚为人说法，和尚一、二度不许，第三度方始得许。院主便欢喜，先报大众，大众喜不自胜，打钟上来。僧众才集，和尚开门便归丈室。院主在外责曰："和尚适来许某甲为人，如今因什么却不为人，赚某甲？"师曰："经师自有经师在，论师自有论师在，律师自有律师在，院主怪贫道什么处？"从此后，从容得数日后，升座便有人问："未审和尚承嗣什么人？"师曰："古佛殿里拾得一行字。"进曰："一行字道什么？"师曰："渠不似我，我不似渠，所以肯这个字。"

李翱相公来见药山和尚，和尚看经次，殊不采顾。相公不肯礼拜，乃发轻言："见面不如千里闻名。"师召相公，相公应喏。师曰："何得贵耳而贱目乎？"相公便礼拜，起来申问："如何是道？"师指天又指地曰："云在青天，水在瓶。"

《祖堂集》

P63　举庞居士辞药山，山命十人禅客相送，至门首，居士指空中雪，云："好雪片片，不落别处。"时有全禅客云："落在什么处？"士打一掌，全云："居士也不得草草。"士云："汝怎么称禅客？阎老子未放汝在。"全云："居士作么生？"士又打一掌，云："眼见如盲，口说如哑。"

《碧岩录》

P64–P65　僧问："久响赵州石桥，到来只是掠彴。"师云："汝只见掠彴，不见赵州桥。"僧云："如何是赵州桥？"师云："过来过来！"又有僧同前问，师亦如前答。僧云："如何是赵州桥？"师云："度驴度马。"僧云："如何是掠彴？"师云："个个度人。"

僧问："学人迷昧，乞师指示。"师云："吃粥也未？"僧云："吃粥也。"师云："洗钵去。"其僧忽然省悟。

《景德传灯录》

P66–P67 夫求法者，应无所求。心外无别佛，佛外无别心。不取善，不舍恶，净秽两边，俱不依怙。达罪性空，念念不可得，无自性故。三界唯心，森罗万象，一法之所印……若体此意，但可随时着衣吃饭，长养圣胎，任运过时，更有何事。（马祖语）

着衣吃饭即表示平常的生活。将平常生活原原本本丝毫不加作为，而任运无作地活下去，就是马祖的禅的生活方式。如果是一般人，则必须加以作为、扭曲才能活下去，亦即平时不断在生活上激起波澜，这就是现实的生活方式。若要虚心而悠悠自适的生活，就必须无心。

问："柏树子还有佛性也无？"师曰："有。"曰："几时成佛？"师曰："待虚空落地时。"曰："几时虚空落地？"师曰："待柏树子成佛时。"

《五灯会元》

P68 僧问："万法归一，一归何所？"师云："老僧在青州，作得一领布衫重七斤。"

《景德传灯录》

P69 僧问赵州："如何是赵州？"州云："东门，西门，南门，北门。"

《碧岩录》

P70 有僧游五台，问一婆子："台山路向什么处去？"婆子云："蓦直恁么去。"僧便去，婆子云："又恁么去也。"其僧举似师。师云："待我去勘破遮婆子。"师至明日，便去问："台山路向什么处去？"婆子云："蓦直恁么去。"师便去。婆子云："又恁么去也。"师归院谓僧曰："我为汝勘破婆子了也。"

《景德传灯录》

P71 问："如何是祖师西来意？"师曰："庭前柏树子。"曰："和尚莫将境示人。"师曰："我不将境示人。"曰："如何是祖师西来意？"师曰："庭前柏树子。"

《五灯会元》

P72–P73 宗教的体验，是以自己来明白自己的，是自身独自得到的绝对境。

赵州和尚六十岁开始学禅，直到八十岁仍在到处参学，那时他已大悟了。他从八十岁开始教学，直到一百二十岁逝世为止。一个学生问他："一物不将来时如何？"赵州答云："放下着！""一物也无，教我放下个什么？""放不下就提取去！"问者于此有省。

"将来"含有"拿来""带来"之意。

《禅话一〇一则》

P74 师问新到："曾到此间么？"曰："曾到。"师曰："吃茶去。"又问僧，僧曰："不曾到。"师曰："吃茶去。"后院主问曰："为什么曾到也云吃茶去，不曾到也云吃茶去？"师召院主，院主应："喏喏！"师曰："吃茶去。"

《五灯会元》

P75–P79 龙潭因德山请益，抵夜，潭云："夜深，子何不下去？"山遂珍重揭帘而出，见外面黑，却回云："外面黑！"潭乃点纸烛度与。山拟接，潭便吹灭。山于此忽然有省，便作礼。潭云："子见个甚么道理？"山云："某甲从今日去不疑天下老和尚舌头也。"至明日，龙潭升座云："可中有个汉，牙如剑树，口似血盆，棒打不回头；他时异日，向孤峰顶上立吾道去在！"山遂取疏钞，于法堂前将一炬火提起云："穷诸玄辩，若一毫致于太虚；竭世枢机，似一滴投于巨壑！"将疏钞便烧，于是礼辞。

无门曰：德山未出关时，心愤愤，口悱悱，得得来南方，要灭却教外别传之旨。及到沣州路上，问婆子买点心。婆云："大德，车子内是什么文字？"山云："金刚经疏钞。"婆云："只如经中道：过去心不可得，现在心不可得，未来心不可得。大德要点哪个心？"德山被者一问，直得口似扁担。然虽如是，未肯向婆子句下死却，遂问婆子："近处有甚宗师？"婆云："五里外有龙潭和尚。"

及到龙潭，纳尽败阙，可谓是前言不应后语！龙潭大似怜儿不觉丑，见他有些子火种时，即忙将恶水蓦头一浇浇杀。

师寻常遇僧到参，多以挂杖打，临济闻之，遣侍者来参，教令："德山若打汝，但接取挂杖，当胸一挂。"侍者到，方礼拜，师乃打，侍者接得挂杖与一挂，师归方丈。侍者回举似临济，济云："从来疑遮个汉。"师上堂曰："问即有过，不问又乖。"有僧出礼拜，师便打，僧曰："某甲始礼拜，为什么便打？"师曰："待汝开口堪作什么！"师令侍者唤义存，（雪峰）存上来，师曰："我自唤存，汝又来什么？"存无对。师因疾，有僧问："还有不病者无？"师曰："有。"问："如何是不病者？"师曰："阿爷阿爷。"

关于禅门的用棒，据祖源禅师在《万法归心录》中归纳有八种："赏棒、罚棒、纵棒、夺棒、愚痴棒、降魔棒、扫迹棒、无情棒。"其实这样的分析未免过细，我们很难把禅门中所有的棒很精确地归入这八种。但就一般来讲，棒的作用，和喝相似，也都是禅师们在不用文字语言的原则下所运用的一种设。（吴怡先生语）

师讳义玄，曹州南华人也，俗姓邢。幼而颖异，及落发受具，志慕禅宗。师在黄檗三年，行业纯一，首座乃叹曰："虽是后生，与众有异"。遂问："上座在此多少时？"师云："三年。"首座云："曾参问也无？"师云："不曾参问，不知问个什么？"首座云："汝何不去问堂头和尚，如何是佛法的大意？"师便去问，声未绝，黄檗便打。师下来，首座云："问话作么生？"师云："某甲问声未绝，和尚便打，某甲不会。"首座云："但更去问！"师又去问，黄檗又打，如是三度发问，三度被打。

《临济录》

P80　有一次，临济禅师上堂对大家说："汝等总学我喝，我今问汝有一人从东堂出，一人从西堂出，两人齐声一喝，者里分得宾主么？汝且作么生分，若分不得已，后不得学老僧喝。"

临济为了防止学人滥用"喝"字，而提出这个公案，主要在于叫人认清主客本是一体，它是无宾无主，就是真正的真我。

事见《指月录》

P81　师（临济义玄）谓僧曰："有时一喝如金刚王宝剑，有时一喝如踞地师子，有时一喝如探竿影草，有时一喝不作一喝用。汝作么生会。"僧拟议，师便喝。

上堂，有僧出礼拜，师便喝，僧云："老和尚，莫探头好！"师云："你道落在什么处？"僧便喝。又有僧问："如何是佛法大意？"师便喝，僧礼拜，师云："你道好喝也无？"僧云："草贼大败。"师云："过在什么处？"僧云："再犯不容。"师云："大众要会临济宾主句，问取堂中二禅客。"便下座。

《五灯会元》

P82　师到初祖塔头，塔主云："长老先礼佛，先礼祖？"师云："佛祖俱不礼塔。"主云："佛祖与长老是什么冤家？"师便拂袖而去。

初祖塔头：塔是梵文坟墓的音译。

《临济录》

P83-P84　潭州渐源仲兴禅师，在道吾处为典座，一日随道吾往檀越家吊丧，师以手拊棺曰："生也死也？"道吾曰："生也不道，死也不道。"师曰："为什么不道？"道吾曰："不道不道！"吊毕同回，途次，师曰："和尚今日须与仲兴道，倘更不道，即打去也。"道吾曰："打即任打，生也不道死也不道。"师遂打道吾数拳。道吾归院，令师且去："少间主事知了打汝。"师乃礼辞往石霜，举前语及打道吾之事请和尚道。石霜曰："汝不见道吾道：'生也不道死也不道？'"师于此大悟。乃设斋忏悔，师一日将锹子于法堂上，从东过西，从西过东。石霜曰："作么？"师曰："觅先师灵骨。"石霜曰："洪波浩渺，白浪滔天，觅什么灵骨？"师曰："正好着力。"石霜曰："这里针扎不入，着什么力？"

《景德传灯录》

P85-P86　婺州金华山俱胝和尚，初住庵，有尼名实际到庵，戴笠子执锡绕师三匝，云："道得，即拈下笠子。"三问，师皆无对，尼便去。师曰："日势稍晚，且留一宿。"尼曰："道得，即宿。"师又无对，尼去后，叹曰："我虽处丈夫之形，而无丈夫之气。"拟弃庵往诸方参寻，其夜山神告曰："不须离此山，将有大菩萨来为和尚说法也。"果旬日，天龙和尚到庵，师乃迎礼，具陈前事天龙竖一指示之，师当下大悟。自此凡有参学僧到，师唯举一指，无别提唱。有一童子于外被人诘曰："和尚说何法要？"童子竖起指头，归而举似师，师以刀断其指头。童子叫唤走出，师召一声，童子回首，师却竖起指头，童子豁然领解。师将顺世，谓众曰："吾得天龙一指头禅，一生用不尽。"言讫，示灭。

《景德传灯录》

P87-P88　用伤害人体的方法以开示佛法，真是一件不可思议的事。假如俱胝没有使童子因此而得开悟的把握，我想他不会如此荒唐。此种动作，绝不是一般人所能效法的：由俱胝的因竖指而得悟、童子的因无指而得悟，可以肯定一点，就是禅师接人，不拘某一种形象。他们是因势利导，具有超越形象的作用。从他们师弟二人开悟的情形分析：俱胝初见尼时，从他自己感叹无丈夫气一语来说，他是着了男女相。所以对尼的问话，不能道得。天然竖起一指，表示在自性上是平等一如的，本无男女之相。一是绝待的象征，所以俱胝因此而得悟。他以后用一指接引学人，也是表示一真绝待之意。但是童子着了竖指的形象，他以为竖起指来才是佛；后来无指可竖，才悟到佛法不在形象之中，所以因此得法。

周中一《禅话》

P89　俱胝和尚，凡有诘问，唯举一指。后有童子，因外人问："和尚说何法要？"童子亦竖指头。胝闻，遂以刃断其指，童子负痛号哭而去。胝复召之，童子回首，胝却竖起指头，童子忽然领悟。胝将顺世，谓众曰："吾得天龙一指头禅，一生受用不尽！"言讫示灭。

无门曰：俱胝并童子悟处不在指头上，若向者里见得，天龙同俱胝并童子与自己一串穿却！颂曰：俱胝钝置老天龙，利刃单提勘小童。巨灵抬手无多子，分破华山千万重！

《无门关》

P90-P91　一日谓众曰："如人在千尺悬崖，口衔树枝，脚无所踏，手无所攀。忽有人问：如何是西来意？若开口答，即丧身失命，若不答，又违他所问。当恁么时，作么生？"

时有招上座出曰："上树时即不问，未上树时如何？"师笑而已。

僧问："祖意教意是同是别？"师曰："鸡寒上树，鸭寒入水。"僧问三乘。

《景德传灯录》

P92-P93　善静在普乐处典园务。有僧辞普乐。普曰："四面是山，阇黎向什么处去？"僧无对。语善静。静代对曰："竹密不妨流水过，山高那阻野云飞。"僧白普乐。普曰："非汝之言。"僧具言园头所教。普乐上堂谓众曰："莫轻园头，他日住一城隍， 五百人常随也。"后果如其言。四面是山，指一切障道逆缘而言。此心大无大相，小无小相。但使心无挂碍，随处可通。僧殆拘于四山之形象，故不能对。

　　有一天，南泉和尚在山上作务时，有位旅僧经过而问道："有名的南泉禅院，不知如何走？"

　　南泉答道："我是花了三十钱买了这把镰刀的。"

　　僧侣又说："我并不是问你镰刀的事，而问你如何到南泉禅院。"

　　南泉答说："这把镰刀使用起来十分锐利。"

事见《葛藤集》

P94-P95　唐朝的李勃是一个有名的读书人，由于读书破万卷，人称之为"李万卷"。有一次，李勃拜访庐山业宗寺的智常和尚，问："在佛典里，有须弥山没入罂粟种子之中的说法，但是，这要从何说起呢？"于是和尚就反问："人称你是李万卷，但是，万卷书怎样装入你这小小的脑袋瓜子里呢？"李勃乃豁然大悟。

　　在《维摩经》《不可思议品》中有"须弥入芥子之中"、"以四大海水入一毛孔"的说法。意即世界的中心妙高山绕行可纳入一颗罂粟子之中，环绕着这座大山的四方之海亦可没入一个毛孔里。

　　昔有一婆子， 供养一庵主经二十年，常使一二八女子送饭给侍。一日，使女子抱曰："正恁么时如何？"主曰："枯木倚寒岩，三冬无暖气。"女子举示婆。婆曰："我二十年，只供养一个俗汉。"

　　终于遣出烧庵。

《指月录》

P96　瑞岩师彦和尚，每日自唤："主人公！"复自应："诺！"乃云："惺惺着！""喏！""他时异日莫受人瞒！""喏！喏！"

　　无门曰：瑞岩老子自买自卖，弄出许多神头鬼面。何故聻？一个唤的，一个应的；一个惺惺的，一个不受人瞒的。认着依前还不是！若也效他，总是野狐见解！颂曰：学道之人不识真，只为从前认识神。无量劫来生死本，痴人唤作本来人！

　　惺惺着：警惕语，清醒些之意。

《无门关》

P97-P98　元和中（八〇六—八一九），白居易出守兹郡，因入山礼谒，乃问师曰："禅师住处甚危险"。师曰："太守危险尤甚。"曰："弟子位镇江山，何险之有？"师曰："薪火相交，识性不停，得非险乎？"

　　又问："如何是佛法大意？"师曰："诸恶莫作， 众善奉行。"白曰："三岁孩儿也解恁么道。"师曰："三岁孩儿虽道得，八十老人行不得。"白遂作礼。

　　有源律师来问："和尚修道，还用功否？"师曰："用功。"曰："如何用功？"师曰："饥来吃饭，困来眠。"曰："一切人总如同师用功否？"师曰："不同。"曰："何故不同？"师曰："他吃饭时不肯吃饭，百种须索；睡时不肯睡，千般计较，所以不同也。"律师杜口。

《景德传灯录》

P99-P100　幽州盘山宝积禅师，一天路过市场，偶然听到如下的一段对话而有所悟：

　　顾客向屠夫说道："精的割一斤来！"

153

屠夫放下屠刀叉手道："老兄，哪个不是精的？"

山谷一日参晦堂和尚，堂云："公所诵书中，有一两句，仲尼曰：'二三子以我为隐乎？吾无隐乎尔！'甚与宗门事恰好也，公知之么？"山谷云："不知。"后晦堂与山谷山行之次，天香满山。堂问曰："公闻木樨花香么？"云："闻。"堂曰："吾无隐乎尔！"山谷释然有省。经两月后，参死心禅师，死心一拶云："长老死，学士死，烧作两堆灰，怎么时向什么处相见？"山拟议，不契。后左官黔南，道力愈胜，于无思念中顿明死心所问，从是得大自在之三昧。

《葛藤集》

P101—P103　至江陵白马寺，堂中遇一老宿，名曰慧勤，师亲近询请。勤曰："吾久侍丹霞，今既垂老，倦于提诱，汝可往谒翠微，彼即吾同参也。"师礼辞而去，造于翠微之堂。问："如何是西来意？"翠微曰："待无人即向汝说。"师良久曰："无人也，请师说。"翠微下禅床引师入竹园，师又曰："无人也，请和尚说。"翠微指竹曰："这竿得恁么长，那竿得恁么短。"师虽领其微言，犹未彻其玄旨。

师谓众云："有一人长不吃饭不道饥，有一人终日吃饭不道饱。"众皆无对。云岩问："和尚每日驱驱为阿谁？"师云："有一人要。"岩云："因什么不教伊自作？"师云："他无家活。"

师煎茶次，道吾问："煎与阿谁？"师曰："有一人要。"曰："何不教伊自煎？"师曰："幸有某甲在。"

《景德传灯录》

P104　镜清问僧："门外是什么声？"僧云："雨滴声！"清云："众生颠倒，迷己逐物。"僧云："和尚作么生？"清云："洎不迷己。"僧云："洎不迷己，意旨如何？"清云："出身犹可易，脱体道应难。"

《碧岩录》

P105—P109　师与韦监军吃果子，韦问："如何是日用而不知？"师（玄沙）拈起果子曰："吃。"韦吃果子了，再问之，师曰："只者是日用而不知"。

思师问希迁曰："子何方而来？"迁曰："曹溪。"师曰："将得什么来？"曰："未到曹溪亦不失。"师曰："恁么用到曹溪作什么？""若不到曹溪，争知不失。"迁又问曰："曹溪大师还识得和尚否？"师曰："汝今识吾否？"曰："识又争能识得。"师曰："众角虽多，一麟足矣。"

禅的源底，究非语言可得表现；禅的真实相，不容有闲言语、闲妄想的余地。除"教外别传，不立文字，直指人心，见性成佛"之外，别无可求之道。不立，即是直示着不容语言文字，原来怎样就是怎样地直接启示着真理。

师住西堂后，有一俗士问："有天堂地狱否？"师曰："有。"曰："有佛法僧宝否？"师曰："有。"更有多问，尽答言有。曰："和尚怎么道莫错否？"师曰："汝曾见曾宿来耶？"曰："某甲曾参径山和尚来。"师曰："径山向汝作么生道？"曰："他道一切总无。"师曰："汝有妻否？"曰："有。"师曰："径山和尚有妻否？"曰："无。"师曰："径山和尚道无即得。"俗士礼谢而去。

师即大悟。唐贞元中，居于大梅山鄞县南七十里梅子真旧隐，时盐官会下一僧入山采柱杖，迷路至庵所问曰："和尚在此山多少时也？"师曰："只见四山青又黄。"又问："出山路向什么处去？"师曰："随流去。"

《景德传灯录》

P111—P112　此处所说的进退，指有空而言，也就是对世法的肯定和否定。执着任何一面，都是不

154

对，有进有退，是是非非两忘，善恶双离的办法，也就是超越是非。

守端有一次对杨岐口述郁和尚的悟道偈："我有明珠一颗，久被尘劳关锁。今朝尘尽光生，照破河山万朵。"杨岐听了笑着走了。守端整夜失眠。次日问杨岐为何大笑。杨答："你不如小丑，小丑喜欢人笑，你却怕人笑。"守端因而大悟。小丑能使人笑，是小丑演技的成功。至于杨岐的笑。有两种看法：一种是因守端转述他人的知见，等于数他家珍宝，与己何益，故此发笑。一种是守端既是欣赏这个偈子，是已领悟心即是佛的道理。所以杨岐笑着走了，好让守端怀疑，继续参究。果然守端苦参一夜以后，灵机活跃；再经杨岐一言，便开悟了。杨岐之言，也暗含着只要自己有了真功夫，笑骂由人，与我何损。正老子所谓："不笑不足为道。"一切但求之在我而已。所谓"自得之则资之深，资之深则取诸左右逢其源"。又何必舍己求人。

周中一《禅话》

P113　唐元和中，（丹霞）至洛京龙门、香山，与伏牛（自在）和尚为莫逆之友。后于慧林寺，遇天大寒，师取木佛焚之，人或讥之。师曰："吾烧取舍利。"人曰："木头何有？"师曰："若尔者，何贵我乎？"

《景德传灯录》

P114-P116　吴怡先生认为：在这则公案里，丹霞以一位禅师的身份，居然亲自烧木佛以取暖，这在一般宗教的眼中，无异是叛教的行为，可是在禅宗的文献里却大书特书，变成了一则著名的公案。究竟是何原因？如果我们依照这则公案的对话来看，问题似乎很简单，因为木佛没有舍利，所以可焚；也就是说木佛只是偶像，没有佛性，所以能烧。这种行为在禅宗的文献里并不稀奇，像呵佛骂祖之事，经常出现。其目的都是要我们打破心中的执着……这种焚木佛的境界固然很高，但其行为却只许丹霞有一次；丹霞自己用多了，或后人盲目地模仿，都将变为狂禅。

僧问扬州石塔宣秘礼禅师："山河大地，与己是同是别？"师曰："长亭凉夜月，多为客铺舒。"一切自然环境，与众生皆有深切的关系。皆能影响众生的生活。故天地并生，万物为一体。

僧问大龙："色身败坏，如何是坚固法身？"龙云："山花开似锦，涧水湛如蓝。"

《碧岩录》

P117-P118　有侍者会通，唐德宗时为六宫使，王族咸美之。七岁蔬食，十一受五戒，二十有二为出家故休官，鸟窠即与披剃，其常卯斋，昼夜精进，诵大乘经而习安般三昧。忽一日，欲辞去，师问曰："汝今何往？"对曰："会通为法出家，以和尚不垂慈诲，今往诸方学佛法去。"师曰："若是佛法，吾此间亦有少许。"曰："如何是和尚佛法？"师于身上拈起布毛吹之，会通遂领悟玄旨。时谓布毛侍者。

师问西堂："汝还解捉得虚空么？"西堂云："捉得！"师云："作么生捉？"堂以手撮虚空师云："作么生恁么捉虚空？"堂却问："师兄作么生捉？"师把西堂鼻孔拽西堂作忍痛声云："大杀拽人鼻孔。"直得脱去师云："直须恁么捉虚空始得。"

《景德传灯录》

P119-P121　在外道问佛的公案（第六十五）中："外道问佛：'不问有言，不问无言。'世尊良久。外道赞叹云：'大慈大悲，开我迷云，令我得入！'外道去后，阿难问佛：'外道有何所证，而言得入？'佛言：'如世良马，见鞭影而行。'"

这个公案外道的问，据语录原文"外道问佛：如何是佛？但不问有言，不问无言"的节记。这个质问就是说：所谓佛，是什么呢？换句话说：释尊大悟的内容，是什么东西呢？意即：不是问超越的要体上

155

有无的说明。盖有无的肯定与否定的论争，不过是局在四句百非圈里抬杠子的玩意儿罢了，所以宁避免闲文，直以要求断定自己的所信为上策，故发出这个问。世尊的本身，即是佛法；超越了有无的肯定与否定的绝对的存在；为示出离有无二边的绝对的存在，示以暂时的沉默；这就是完全地呈露出现成自体的佛法的姿态。

乾峰和尚因僧问："十方薄伽梵，一路涅槃门。未审路头在什么处？"峰拈起拄杖划一划云："在这里！"后僧请益云门，门拈起扇子云："扇子踍跳上三十三天，筑着帝释鼻孔，东海鲤鱼打一棒，雨似盆倾！"

无门曰：一人向深深海底行，簸土扬尘；一人于高高山顶立，白浪滔天。把定放行，各出一只手扶竖宗乘，大似两个驼子相撞着，世上应无直的人。正眼观来，二大老总未识路头在。

《无门关》

P122　僧问："寒暑到来，如何回避？"师云："何不向无寒暑处去？"云："如何是无寒暑处？"师云："寒时寒杀阇黎，热时热杀阇黎。"

投子同云："几乎与么去。"

《洞山录》

P123　尼众问："如何得为僧去？"师曰："作尼来多少时也？"尼曰："还有为僧时也无？"师曰："汝即今是什么？"尼曰："现是尼身，何得不识？"师曰："谁识汝？"

《景德传灯录》

P124　洞山和尚因僧问："如何是佛？"山云："麻三斤！"

无门曰：洞山老人参得些蚌蛤禅，才开两片，露出肝肠。然虽如是，且道：向什么处见洞山？颂曰：突出麻三斤，言亲意更亲。来说是非者，便是是非人！

蚌蛤禅：言其禅直接明白，如蚌蛤一般，才一开口，便表露无遗也。

突然提出"麻三斤"来答"如何是佛"的问话，此答不但言语亲切，而且意思亦更加的亲切，毫无隔阂。此事没有是非可说，来说是非的人，便是惹是生非的人了。

《无门关》

P125　宇宙万有，是无常的，也是无始无终地存在着。现象即实在，眼见耳闻都是佛。僧问"如何是佛"，答之以"麻三斤"，也是举其一例罢了。这个公案语，不是这样就完结。僧于洞山之答不能理解，再举以问智门。智门答以"花簇簇，锦簇簇"，转问僧曰："会不会？"僧说："不会。"因之更说云："南地竹兮北地木。"这是说：黄花、红叶、竹、木、无不是佛。由此类推三斤麻，亦自然是佛了。

芝峰法师译《禅学讲话》

P126　五祖曰："譬如水牯牛过窗棂，头、角、四蹄都过了，因什么尾巴过不得？"

无门曰：若向者里颠倒着一只眼，下得一转语，可以上报四恩，下资三有。其或未然，更须照顾尾巴始得！颂曰：

过去堕坑堑，回来却被坏。

这些尾巴子，直是甚奇怪！

《无门关》

P127 琅玡觉和尚语录："先圣道：'有物先天地，无形本寂寥，能为万物主，不逐四时调'。好个颂，却成两橛。若有人检点得出，许你一只眼。"前两句说的是体，第三句说的是用。体用分离，所以说是成了两橛。体用本是不可分的。分成两橛，则非自性；只是识心中有对待的事物。觉师教人检点的，当是最后一句。"四时调"三字是指用而言。上面用"不逐"二字予以否定，是就体而言。一句中有动有静，体用兼摄，而又相即相离，真是活泼泼的自性，只此五字，说明了体用的超越性。

周中一《禅话》

P128—P131 《景德传灯录》另有一则"万古长空，一朝风月"的对话：

问："达摩未来此土时，还有佛法也无。"师（天柱崇慧）曰："未来时且置，即今事作么生？"曰："某甲不会，乞师指示？"师曰："万古长空，一朝风月。"良久又曰："阇黎会么？自己分上作么生，干他达摩与未来作么？"

吴怡先生对此则公案有如下的说法：所谓万古长空，就是指的佛法无边，无过去、现在、未来，这是真空。所谓一朝风月乃指天地间任何事物，都有其当体的存在，这是妙有。但真空即妙有，妙有即真空，万古是一朝，一朝也是万古，所以天柱不谈"未来"，而只问"今事"，因为"今事"能明，即通未来。而当下能悟，即是佛性，还管他达摩的来与未来。

沩山灵佑将入灭时语众云："老僧百年后向山下做一头水牯牛，左胁书五字云'沩山僧某甲'。此时唤作沩山僧，又是水牯牛，唤做水牯牛，又是沩山僧。到底唤做什么即得？"一个人在将死之时，生理上的痛苦，心理上的悲哀，都是免不了的。在此千钧一发之际的生死关头，居然能够谈笑自若。此种超越生死的达观态度，实足令人惊奇。但令人惊奇的还不在此。尤其是他把自己和水牯牛搭在一起。乍然一听他的怪论，会使你啼笑皆非。我们再仔细地一推敲，也就觉得平淡无奇。因为沩山僧与水牯牛本为大自然不可分的一体。一个人只要没有能所的分别心，便能超越自他，超越物我。不仅人与人间，无自他之分，乃至人与畜间，亦无自他之分。一个禅人到此境地，已是外形骸，一生死，所以能够从容坐化。

周中一《禅话》

P132—137 大梅问马祖云："什么是佛？"马祖答："即心即佛。"大梅言下便悟。后来马祖派一个僧人去考验大梅。僧问大梅："你在马祖门下学到些什么？"大梅回答："马祖教我即心即佛。"僧云："现在马祖已改变了，说非心非佛。"大梅云："这个老和尚作弄人没有了期。管他什么非心非佛，我只管即心即佛。"僧人归语马祖。马祖便说："梅子熟了。"是指大梅已彻悟而言。这段公案说明学人不能执着肯定或否定一面，要有一种超越是非的精神，才是彻悟。宗宝云："即心即佛，表语也；非心非佛，遮语也。今人多重遮语，谓无痕迹，而忽表语。不知即心即佛，唯过量大人，方能担荷。"又云："二祖觅心不可得，达摩云：'与汝安心竟。'与此同一鼻孔。"宗宝所说的表语，即指肯定而言；遮语指否定而言。大梅的表语，正表示能够担荷的过量大人。所以马祖说他成熟了。

一天，释迦牟尼独自在极乐世界的莲花池畔信步走着。池塘中绽放着的莲花，宛若玉石一般晶莹可爱。一种无以形容的芳香，从花蕊里不绝地向外飘漾着。此刻的极乐世界正是清晨。

不一会儿，释迦伫立在池畔，从覆盖于水面的莲叶隙间，无意中看到池底下的情景。这极乐世界的莲池下面，正是地狱的底层，因而透过水晶般莹澈的水，宛如透过透视镜一般，可以清楚地看到奈河和针山的情形。

这时，地狱底层，一个叫犍陀多的汉子和别的罪人一起蠢动的模样，落进释迦的佛眼里。这个叫犍陀多的汉子，过去虽是个杀人放火干尽坏事的大盗，却也做过一件——唯一的一件善事。事情是这样的，有一次，当他穿过森林的时候，发现一只小蜘蛛在路旁爬行，犍陀多随即抬起脚来，想踩死它，却又突然改变了主意，他想："不行，不行，蜘蛛虽小，也是有生命的。要是滥杀了它，也是怪可怜的。"终于饶了蜘蛛的命。

释迦牟尼一面浏览地狱的情景，一面记起犍陀多曾经放过蜘蛛的事。他想尽可能地把这汉子救出地狱，以酬报他的善行。释迦往旁边一望，正好发现翡翠色的莲叶上，悬垂着一根极乐世界的蜘蛛吐出的美丽的银丝。他便轻轻拈起那根蜘蛛丝，从玉一般晶莹的白莲隙间，笔直地垂入深邃的地狱底层。

这儿是地狱底层的血池，犍陀多跟其他的罪人在那儿乍浮乍沉着。到处都是暗黑一片，偶尔朦胧隐现的亮光，也是令人不寒而栗的针山上闪烁的针光。那种恐怖是无以言宣的。加之，周遭宛似坟地那般死寂，偶尔听到的，也只是罪人吐出的恢弱的叹息。沉沦在这儿的罪人，都已遭到地狱的种种折磨而疲累不堪，连哭出声的气力都丧尽了。即使是大盗犍陀多，也在血池里哽咽着，犹如濒死的青蛙一味地扭动着身体……

芥川龙之介《蜘蛛之丝》

P138—P141　一天薄暮，一个佣工正站在罗生门下躲雨。

宽敞的城门下，除他没有第二个人了。仅有一只蟋蟀，停在处处红漆斑剥了的大圆柱上。罗生门既在朱雀大路上，照理该有几个戴高顶女笠或软头巾的人在那里躲雨，而竟除了他没有第二个人。

这是近年来，京都因为地震、旋风、大火、饥馑等天灾人祸接踵而来，使京中寥落得迥异寻常。据旧志上的记载：佛像或供具被敲碎了，那些油漆或贴金的木头堆积在路边，被当作柴薪来出售。京中的情况如此，罗生门的修缮当然也搁在一边，当然谁也懒得去管了。而看中了这里的荒凉，狐狸来此藏身，盗贼来此栖止，到后来甚至没有人认的死尸，也被送到这个城楼上来抛弃了。因而到了日色西沉，即令人毛骨悚然，谁也不敢到这城门附近来走动了。

倒是不知道从哪里飞来的许多乌鸦，都齐集到这里来。白天，不知道有多少，在空中画着圆圈，绕着高跷着的鸱尾，边叫边飞翔。当罗生门的上空被晚霞染上一片红色时，它们像是撒着芝麻一般，尤为清晰。乌鸦，当然是啄楼上的死人肉来的。——但今天，也许是时刻已晚，一只也看不到了。只是处处快要塌倒的，那些裂缝里长着青草的石阶上，这里那里留下来鸦粪的许多白点。佣工在共有九级石阶的最上一级，把洗褪了颜色的蓝夹袄垫在屁股下，一面关心着右颊上那颗偌大青春痘，茫然望着两脚。

刚才作者虽说"佣工在躲雨"，但雨便停了，他也没有什么特别的去处。平时，该是回主人家的时候，但四五天前，他被那个主人解雇了。上面曾说过的，当时京都市面的衰微无以复加。现在这个佣工被多年雇佣的主人解雇，事实上只是这个衰微的小小余波罢了。所以与其说"佣工在躲雨"，倒不如说"被雨赶着的佣工，前途茫茫无处可去"来得恰当。再加上今天的天色，对于这个平安朝的佣工的感伤之情也影响匪浅。从申刻开始落的雨，迄无停止的模样。于是，佣工比什么都迫切的，便是明天的生活如何打发……

要使一筹莫展的事打开僵局，不让你有选择手段的余裕。倘或选择，唯有饿死在泥墙脚下或路边的泥涂中。之后，被送到这个城楼上，像狗一般地被抛弃罢了。倘或不择手段——佣工的想法，在同一条路上不知低徊了多少次，好不容易才到达了这个僻角。但这"倘或"，永远地，结局还是"倘或"。佣工虽是肯定了不择手段，为了给这"倘或"下个论断，跟着而来的必然的结果便是"除非做贼"，但他却鼓不起勇气来作积极的肯定……

芥川龙之介小说《罗生门》

159

菩提本无树
明镜亦非台
本来无一物
何处惹尘埃

Wisdom has never been a tree
And the bright mirror has no stand
There has never been anything
So whereupon can the dust land

六祖坛经
曹溪的佛唱
Zen Masters Of Old
The Quest For Enlightenment

公元五二七年梁大通元年……
In the year 527, the first year of the Datong reign of the Liang dynasty...

菩提达摩和尚坐船来到中国。
A monk from India named Bodhidharma arrived at the shores of southern China.

1
九月二十一日，他在广州上岸。
On the 21st day of the 9th month, he came ashore in Guangzhou (Canton).

2
这时中国的梁武帝是个非常喜欢佛法的皇帝，平时经常着佛衣，吃斋念佛。
At the same time, Emperor Wu of the Liang dynasty was himself infatuated with Buddhism. He often wore Buddhist clothes, ate vegetarian meals, and chanted Buddhist scriptures.

3
同年十月一日达摩受梁武帝之邀到达首都南京。
On the first day of the tenth month of the same year, Bodhidharma accepted Emperor Wu's invitation to the capital at Nanjing.

4
我自即位以来，供养佛僧，建造寺庙，抄写佛经，这究竟有多大功德？
Ever since my ascending the throne, I have supported monks, built temples and monasteries, and copied the scriptures. How many merits shall I receive for this?

这根本没有功德可言。
None to speak of.

5
你所做的只是一点世俗的小果报而已，谈不上真功德。
These are but minor earthly achievements. They are worth no merits.

6
真功德是最圆融纯净的智慧，它的本体是空寂的，你不可能用世俗的方法去得到它。
True merit is the most perfect and pure wisdom, the original substance of which is emptiness and quiescence. You cannot obtain it by earthly means.

7 十月十九日，达摩自知跟梁武帝法缘不合，就从梁渡过长江进入北魏。
On the 19th day of the 10th month, Bodhidharma, realizing his differences with Emperor Wu, departed Liang and crossed the Yangtze river into Northern Wei.

天竺来的高僧现在住在哪里？
Where is that high monk from India living now?

8

他渡江到北魏去了。
He went across the river into Northern Wei.

9

他是什么人呢？
Who is he?

他就是传佛心之印的观世音菩萨。
None other than the bodhisattva Avalokiteśvara, transmitter of the buddha-mind.

10

陛下真是见其人而没能看见，会其人而没能会见。
Your majesty really is one who looks but does not see; meets but does not recognize.

11

12

我确实是见其人而不能见；会其人而不能会啊……
Oh, I am indeed one who looks but does not see, meets but does not recognize...

派赵光文到长江对岸追达摩祖师吧！
Send Zhao Guangwen to the other side of the Yangtze to find him!

没有用啊……即使全国人去追，他也不会回来的。
It's no use... Even if all the people of the country were to pursue him, he would not return.

13

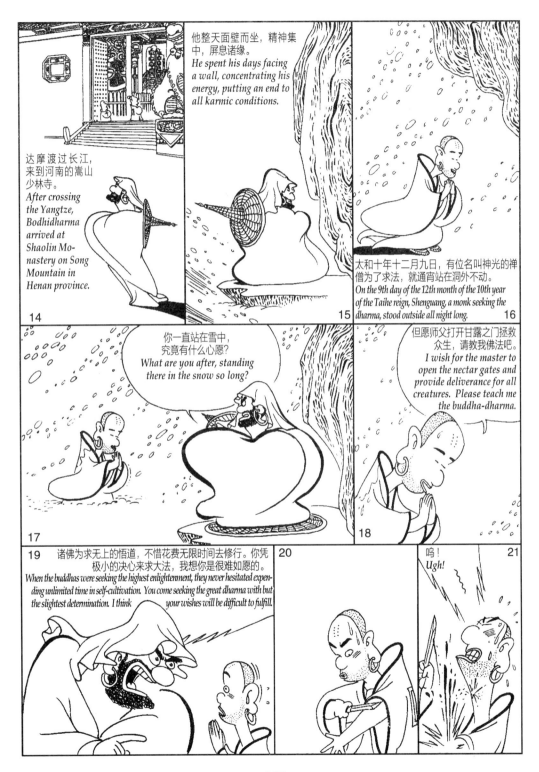

14

达摩渡过长江，来到河南的嵩山少林寺。
After crossing the Yangtze, Bodhidharma arrived at Shaolin Monastery on Song Mountain in Henan province.

他整天面壁而坐，精神集中，屏息诸缘。
He spent his days facing a wall, concentrating his energy, putting an end to all karmic conditions.

15

太和十年十二月九日，有位名叫神光的禅僧为了求法，就通宵站在洞外不动。
On the 9th day of the 12th month of the 10th year of the Taihe reign, Shenguang, a monk seeking the dharma, stood outside all night long.

16

17

你一直站在雪中，究竟有什么心愿？
What are you after, standing there in the snow so long?

但愿师父打开甘露之门拯救众生，请教我佛法吧。
I wish for the master to open the nectar gates and provide deliverance for all creatures. Please teach me the buddha-dharma.

18

19 诸佛为求无上的悟道，不惜花费无限时间去修行。你凭极小的决心来求大法，我想你是很难如愿的。
When the buddhas were seeking the highest enlightenment, they never hesitated expending unlimited time in self-cultivation. You come seeking the great dharma with but the slightest determination. I think your wishes will be difficult to fulfill.

20

呜！
Ugh!

21

28
公元五三六年达摩觉得应该离去了，便召集弟子。
In the year 536, Bodhidharma, feeling that it was time for him to leave, called together his disciples.

29
你们谈谈自己的悟境吧。
I want each of you to tell me about your progress towards enlightenment.

30
我们应该不执着文字，也不舍弃文字，要把文字当作一种求道的工具来运用。
We shouldn't cling to language, yet we shouldn't dispense with it either. We should take language as a useful tool in the quest for enlightenment.

31
你只得到我的皮。
You have attained but my skin.

32
依我所了解的，就像庆喜看到了阿佛国，一见便不再见。
From what I understand, it is like taking joy in seeing the land of the Buddha Aksobhya — once you get a glimpse, you needn't look again.

33
你只得到我的肉。
You have attained but my flesh.

僧璨大集众生，广施正法之雨，这时有位少年僧侣前来膜拜。 **48**
One day when Sengcan had gathered his disciples together to teach the dharma, a young monk stepped forward.

49 什么心才算是佛心呢？
What kind of mind can be considered buddha-mind?

你现在的心是什么心？
What kind of mind is your present mind?

我现在没有心。
Right now I am of no-mind.

连你都没有心了，佛又如何能有心呢？
If you don't have a mind, why would the Buddha have a mind?

50 51

但愿师父能指示一条解脱的法门。
I would appreciate it if you could point out a method of release.

谁绑住了你？
Who tied you up?

没有人绑住我。
No one tied me up.

52 53

既然谁也没绑住你，那你就是已经解脱，为何还要求解脱法门呢？
Then why do you need a method of release?

55 这位和尚当下大悟，他就是禅宗的四祖道信。
With this, the monk achieved enlightenment and went on to become the fourth patriarch of Zen Buddhism, Daoxin.

54

四祖道信
Fourth Patriarch, Daoxin

四祖道信传五祖弘忍，再由五祖将衣钵传给六祖慧能。
The fourth patriarch Daoxin was succeeded by Hongren, the fifth patriarch, who then passed on the robe and almsbowl to Huineng, the sixth patriarch.

五祖弘忍
Fifth Patriarch, Hongren

六祖慧能
Sixth Patriarch Huineng

56

57

六祖慧能可称为中国禅的祖师，由他展开了生气蓬勃的中国禅宗。
The sixth patriarch Huineng can be called the true patriarch of Zen in China, as it was he who was responsible for the vibrancy and flourishing of Chinese Zen Buddhism.

菩提本无树，
明镜亦非台；
本来无一物，
何处惹尘埃？
*Wisdom has never been a tree,
And the bright mirror has no stand;
There has never been anything,
So whereupon can the dust land?*

58

天才是不世出的, 六祖慧能便是这样一位天才, 他和老子、庄子、孔子、孟子都是同一流的伟人。

True geniuses are not of this world. The sixth patriarch Huineng was this kind of genius. He, Laozi (Lao-tzu), Zhuangzi (Chuang-tzu), Confucius, and Mencius were great men of the same strain.

59

他的思想言行被弟子编成了《六祖坛经》一书。这是中国和尚所写, 唯一被奉为《经》的伟大佛学著作。

His thinking, his words, and his actions were compiled by disciples into a short book called the Platform Sutra of the Sixth Patriarch, the only Chinese Buddhist work to attain the status of a sacred scripture.

六祖壇经
Platform Sūtra

60

坛经是一本出自一位真人的肺腑之言, 一字一句都像活泉所喷出的泉水一样清新入骨。

The Platform Sutra is a heartfelt book generated by a truly genuine person. Every word, every sentence, is as fresh and penetrating as water from a clear spring.

六祖慧能
The Sixth
Patriarch
Huineng

1
慧能俗姓卢，生于公元六三八年，广东岭南人。
Huineng's lay surname was Lu, and he was born in the year 638 in Guangdong province.

2
父亲很早就死了，家境很清苦，平常依靠卖柴为生。
His father died while Huineng was still young, leaving the family in poverty, but coming from an honest and hard-working home, Huineng supported himself by peddling fire-wood.

3
也因此而没有机会读书写字。
It was also because of this that he never had the opportunity to attend school.

大学之道在明明德。
The Way of great learning is in illuminating luminous virtue.

4
送柴火来了。
Here's your firewood.

那边放着就成，钱给你。
Just put it right there, and here's the money.

5

174

在弘忍的众多弟子当中，神秀上座是大家公认最有希望接传衣钵的人。
Among Hongren's disciples, one Shenxiu was recognized by all to be the one most likely to receive the robe and almsbowl.

身是菩提树
心如明镜台
时时勤拂拭
莫使惹尘埃
The body is the wisdom tree,
The mind like a bright mirror stand;
Always strive to wipe it clean,
Making sure that no dust lands.

棒。
Wonderful.

对。
Yes.

好。
Merveilleux

身是菩提树，心如明镜台；时时勤拂拭，莫使惹尘埃！
The body is the wisdom tree, The mind like a bright mirror stand; Always strive to wipe it clean, Making sure that no dust lands!

这首偈子是谁作的？
Who wrote that?

是神秀作的，写在墙上。
Shenxiu. He wrote it on the wall.

带我去看行吗？
Can you take me to see it?

好。
OK.

身是菩提树
心如明镜台
时时勤拂拭
莫使惹尘埃
The body is the wisdom tree,
The mind like a bright mirror stand;
Always strive to wipe it clean,
Making sure that no dust lands.

偈子就写在这里。
Here it is.

啊。
Oh.

42

有情来下种，
因地果还生；
无情亦无种，
无性也无生。

A sentient being plants a seed,
Because of soil it returns to life;
Without sentience, there are no seeds,
Without self-nature, there is no life.

慧能得五祖传衣钵之后，
就一直往南走。

Upon receiving the robe and alms-
bowl from Hongren, Huineng headed
south and just kept going.

43 44

我的衣钵已经南传，能者得之。

My robe and almsbowl have
been transmitted southward.
An able (neng) person has re-
ceived them.

45 46

能者得之，那不就是
慧能得了吗?

"An able person."
That must mean
Huineng got them!

南蛮子也能得衣钵?

Can a southern barba-
rian be recipient of the
robe and almsbowl?

49

然而，慧能已埋名隐姓潜居江南，谁也找不到他了，直到十五年后……
But Huineng had already gone incognito in the southern countryside. No one could find him, until fifteen years later...

65 接着印宗便替慧能落发受戒。
Following this, Yinzong shaved Huineng's head and formally ordained him.

66 自己反而拜六祖慧能为师。
And then he himself took Huineng as his teacher.

67 第二年，六祖慧能来到曹溪地方，由许多信徒支持，建立了宝林寺，他就在这寺中开始传法。
The following year, Huineng went to the area near the Cao river and, through the support of his many followers, constructed Baolin monastery. It was here that he began spreading the dharma.

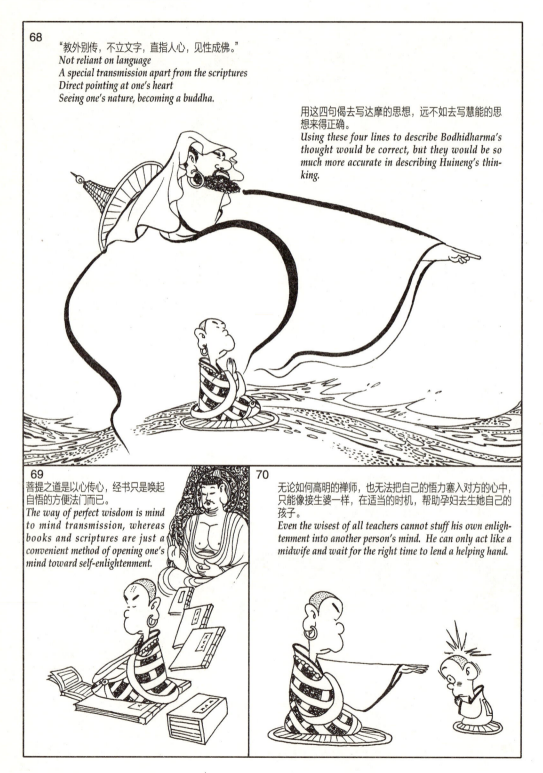

68

"教外别传，不立文字，直指人心，见性成佛。"
Not reliant on language
A special transmission apart from the scriptures
Direct pointing at one's heart
Seeing one's nature, becoming a buddha.

用这四句偈去写达摩的思想，远不如去写慧能的思想来得正确。
Using these four lines to describe Bodhidharma's thought would be correct, but they would be so much more accurate in describing Huineng's thinking.

69

菩提之道是以心传心，经书只是唤起自悟的方便法门而已。
The way of perfect wisdom is mind to mind transmission, whereas books and scriptures are just a convenient method of opening one's mind toward self-enlightenment.

70

无论如何高明的禅师，也无法把自己的悟力塞入对方的心中，只能像接生婆一样，在适当的时机，帮助孕妇去生她自己的孩子。
Even the wisest of all teachers cannot stuff his own enlightenment into another person's mind. He can only act like a midwife and wait for the right time to lend a helping hand.

不立文字
Not
Reliant
On
Language
language

1 我们不应执着于经中的文字，也不应认为别人依照我们的话便能解脱。
We should not cling to the words in the scriptures, and we shouldn't think that others can attain release by relying on our words.

2 应该"自性真空，但可别执着于空"。如果静坐时使自己的心完全空掉了，那便是槁木死灰的顽空。
One should "make one's nature genuinely empty", yet not cling to emptiness. If you completely empty your mind while meditating, it will be just a foolish emptiness, dead and withered.

3 真空就是无限的真实，万法都在人的心中。
Genuine emptiness is limitless truth. The myriad dharmas are in one's mind.

空 Empty 空 Empty 空 Empty 空 Empty

4 执着于空的人，常常诽谤经书，主张抛弃一切文字。
Someone who clings to emptiness often slanders the scriptures and favors forsaking all forms of language.

5 如果真的抛弃文字，那么连"不立文字"的话也应该抛弃，因为这句话也着了文字相。
If we were to really forsake all language, then we would even have to forsake the line "not reliant on language", since this is also language.

思想是没有声音的语言，而文字则是语言的符号。过多的语言和思虑，反而与根本智不相应了。
Thought is a language without sound, and words are the symbols of language. Too much language or thought, however, is not compatible with fundamental wisdom.

直指人心
Direct Pointing At One's Mind

1
由于心，我们才能实现自我，由于心，我们才会步入地狱。
It is only through the mind that we can realize the self. It is only through the mind that we would step into hell.

2
没有心，便没有善与恶、舍与执、迷与悟、菩提与烦恼。
Without the mind, there is neither good nor evil, forsaking or clinging to, confusion or enlightenment, perfect wisdom or distress.

3
心不是静的整体，而是动的历程，像水一样，有时纯净，有时混浊，有时平稳，有时急湍。
Mind is not a static entity, but rather, a process in motion, like water. Sometimes it is pure, other times turbid; sometimes it is still, other times it rushes along.

4
心的悟力是常流的，而不停于一处。
The mind's power of enlightenment is always flowing and never stops in one place.

5
应无所住而生其心，不染着于物，为物所奴役驱使，于是心便解脱了。
"Abiding in nothing, let the mind come through." Do not be sullied by material things or let material things enslave you or order you around. In this way, the mind will gain release.

道是使我们能逍遥自在的，可是偏执的心却使外界的一切变成了我们的桎梏。
The Dao can make us carefree, but a mind that insists on clinging to things turns the outside world into one's own shackles.

见性成佛
Seeing One's Nature, Becoming a Buddha

1
一般人认为明、暗两者不同，但有智慧的人却了解明、暗两者的本性是没有差别的。
Most people think that light and darkness are different, but a wise person understands that the original natures of light and darkness are the same.

2
我们的自性本是清净的，为善为恶都是由心而生。
Our self-natures were originally pure. Goodness and badness arose from our minds.

3
如果此心想恶的话，便入地狱。
If the mind thinks of bad things, then one descends into hell.

4
想善的话，便进天堂。
If one thinks of good things, then one ascends to heaven.

5
有恶害之心，便变为龙蛇；有慈悲之心，便变为菩萨。
A wicked mind becomes a vile serpent. A merciful mind becomes a bodhisattva.

执迷不悟，念念起恶便无法得道。一念向善，便生智慧，想通了你即是"佛"。
A mind stuck in confusion constantly gives rise to badness and will therefore never be enlightened. One thought toward goodness gives rise to wisdom, thus allowing one to realize buddhahood.

6
明暗、有无、善恶、生死都是相对的，"自性"是超越相对，却又包含相对，能达到这点你便是"自性化身佛"。
Light and darkness, being and nothingness, goodness and badness, and life and death are all relative. "Self-nature" transcends relativity yet includes it. If you can comprehend this, you will be able to transform your own nature into a buddha.

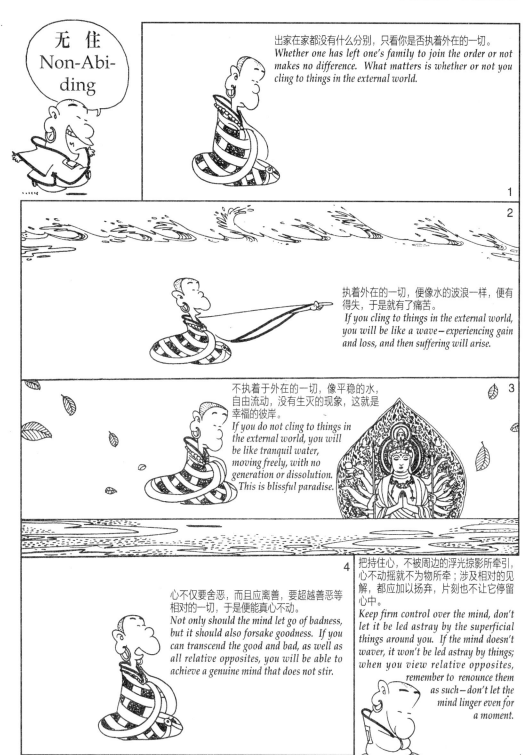

无住
Non-Abi-ding

1
出家在家都没有什么分别，只看你是否执着外在的一切。
Whether one has left one's family to join the order or not makes no difference. What matters is whether or not you cling to things in the external world.

2
执着外在的一切，便像水的波浪一样，便有得失，于是就有了痛苦。
If you cling to things in the external world, you will be like a wave—experiencing gain and loss, and then suffering will arise.

3
不执着于外在的一切，像平稳的水，自由流动，没有生灭的现象，这就是幸福的彼岸。
If you do not cling to things in the external world, you will be like tranquil water, moving freely, with no generation or dissolution. This is blissful paradise.

4
心不仅要舍恶，而且应离善，要超越善恶等相对的一切，于是便能真心不动。
Not only should the mind let go of badness, but it should also forsake goodness. If you can transcend the good and bad, as well as all relative opposites, you will be able to achieve a genuine mind that does not stir.

把持住心，不被周边的浮光掠影所牵引，心不动摇就不为物所牵；涉及相对的见解，都应加以扬弃，片刻也不让它停留心中。
Keep firm control over the mind, don't let it be led astray by the superficial things around you. If the mind doesn't waver, it won't be led astray by things; when you view relative opposites, remember to renounce them as such—don't let the mind linger even for a moment.

南顿北渐
Sudden In the South, Gradual In the North

1

这时，以唐都长安为中心而盛行的是神秀之教，俗称"北宗"。

With the Tang capital of Changan as its center of activity, the teachings of Shenxiu flourished and became known as the "Northern Sect".

渐悟
Gradual Enlightenment

与此对立的慧能之教就被称为"南宗"。北宗神秀唱渐悟；南宗慧能重顿悟，于是展开了禅宗的南北对抗。

In contrast to this, Huineng's teachings became known as the "Southern Sect". Shenxiu of the Northern Sect promoted gradual enlightenment, while Huineng of the Southern Sect emphasized sudden enlightenment. Thus arose the Northern versus Southern schism in Zen.

顿悟
Sudden Enlightenment

2

3

在慧能门下，有五位学生最为突出，他们就是：
南岳怀让　青原行思　永嘉玄觉　南阳慧忠　荷泽神会

Among Huineng's disciples, there were five who stood out among the rest. They were:
Nanyue Huairang
Qingyuan Xingsi
Yongjia Xuanjue
Nanyang Huizhong
Heze Shenhui

南岳怀让
Huairang Of Nanyue

陕西金州人，俗姓杜。十五岁出家先学律宗，后来不满所学，便到嵩山拜慧安为师，慧安介绍他到曹溪去见慧能。

From Jin prefecture in Shaanxi province, his lay surname was Du. He left his family for the order at fifteen and first studied the Vinaya Sect. Unsatisfied, however, he went to Song Mountain to study under Huaian, who suggested he go to Caoxi (Cao river) to study under Huineng.

你的看法正好和我的相同，这个不会污染的，乃是佛、菩萨要我们留心维护的。
Your views are the same as mine. That which wouldn't be defiled is that which the buddhas and bodhisattvas wish us to be mindful of protecting.

怀让便在慧能门下，跟随问学了十五年。
So Huairang took his place as Huineng's disciple and studied with him for fifteen years.

他后来便到了南岳，大大地弘扬禅学。
He then went to Nanyue, where he succeeded in greatly disseminating Zen.

他的弟子中最有名的就是"马祖道一"。
His most famous disciple was Mazu Daoyi.

青原行思
Xingsi Of Qingyuan

江西吉川人，俗姓刘，自小出家，赋性沉默。
From Ji prefecture in Jiangxi province, his lay surname was Liu. He left home to join the order at a very young age and he was of a quiet disposition.

1

我们要怎样才不涉入相对的层次中？
What can we do to keep from slipping into the levels of relativism?

在他初见六祖时，问道：
At his first meeting with Huineng, he asked:

2 你最近做了些什么功夫？
What works have you done lately?

3 我连圣谛也没有修过。
I haven't even worked on the sacred truth.

4 那么你的功夫到达哪一个层次？
And what level has this work brought you to?

5 我连圣谛也不修，还有什么层次可言？
If I haven't even worked on the sacred truth, what level is there to speak of?

好好好！很好！
Good, good. Very good!

6 慧能被他的见地感动，认为他是学生中最有成就的一个。
Huineng was impressed by his depth and regarded him as having accomplished the most of all of his students.

后来他被派到吉州青原山去弘法，发扬了慧能的道统。
Later, Xingsi was sent to Quingyuan Mountain in Ji prefecture to spread the dharma. There, he disseminated the orthodox teachings of Huineng.

他也只有一位杰出的弟子，就是石头希迁。
He had only one outstanding disciple, Shitou Xiqian.

虽只一位，但已足够了，众角虽多，一麟足矣。
Although he was but one, he was sufficient. "Though horns are numerous, a unicorn suffices."

永嘉玄觉
Xuanjue Of Yongjia

俗姓戴，浙江永嘉人，初学天台宗，曾潜心于禅观，后来到慧能处印证所学。

From Yongjia in Zhejiang province, his lay surname was Dai. He initially studied the Tiantai sect and was accomplished in meditation. Later he went to the place of Huineng to verify what he had learned.

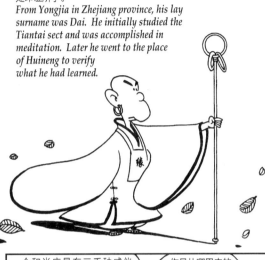

初见慧能时，他绕着慧能走了三圈。

At their first meeting, Xuanjue walked three circles around Huineng.

一个和尚应具有三千种威仪、八万种戒行。

A monk should have three thousand kinds of dignified deportment and eighty thousand kinds of refined behavior.

你是从哪里来的，竟然如此傲慢无礼？

Where are you from and why are you so bold and brash?

人的生死只在呼吸之间，万物变化很快，我顾不了这么多。

Life is but a breath. Everything changes so fast. How can I pay attention to it all?

既然担心生死，为何不证取不生不灭的大道，去除烦恼呢？

If you're so worried about life, why don't you experience the great Dao, which transcends both rebirth and speed, and thereby be rid of all your troubles?

南阳慧忠
Huizhong Of Nanyang

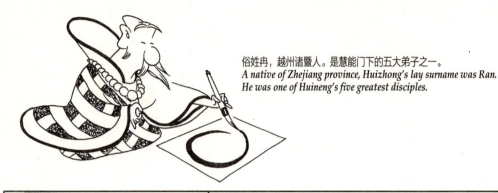

俗姓冉，越州诸暨人。是慧能门下的五大弟子之一。
A native of Zhejiang province, Huizhong's lay surname was Ran.
He was one of Huineng's five greatest disciples.

1

他在慧能处印证了以后，便到南阳的白崖山度了四十余年，从未离山一步。
After studying under Huineng, he went to Baiya Mountain in Nanyang, where he lived for more than forty years, not once stepping foot off the mountain.

2

公元七六一年，肃宗邀请他到京城，尊为国师。
In the year 761, Emperor Suzong invited him to the capital to accept the post of National Teacher.

3

在一次法会上，肃宗向他问了很多问题，他却不看肃宗一眼。
Once during a meeting with the emperor, although the emperor asked many questions, Huizhong refused to even look at him.

荷泽神会
Shenhui Of Heze

神会是湖北襄阳人，俗姓高。他对维护慧能的法统及使禅宗通俗化的贡献很大，并使得提倡顿悟的南禅，压倒了渐悟的北禅。

From Xiangyang in Hubei province, Shenhui's lay surname was Gao. He made great strides in protecting Huineng's orthodoxy and in popularizing Zen. He also ensured that the Southern Sect of sudden enlightenment surpassed in popularity the Northern Sect of gradual enlightenment.

他十三岁时便去参拜慧能。
Shenhui first studied under Huineng when he was only thirteen.

你千里跋涉而来，是否带着你最根本的东西？
Having come from so far away, did you bring your most fundamental thing?

1

如果带来了，那么你应该知道它的主体是什么，你说说看。
If yes, you should know what its most important aspect is. See if you can tell me.

2 这东西就是无住，它的主体就是开眼即看。
This thing of which you speak is non-abiding. It's most important aspect is opening one's eyes and seeing.

你这小和尚，词锋倒也敏利。
For such a young monk, you're pretty sharp.

3

师父坐禅时，是见或是不见？
Master, when you meditate, do you see or not?

4

5 bonk bonk bonk!

我打你，是痛或是不痛？
When I hit you, does it hurt or not?

我很清楚自己要去哪里，不然我又如何能预先告诉你们？
I know well where I am going. How else would I be able to tell you ahead of time?

18

你们哭泣是因为不知我死后往哪里去，如果知道了便不会哭泣的。
You are all crying because you don't know where I'm going. If you knew, you wouldn't cry.

19

你们要知道，法性是不会生灭去来的。
The dharma-nature can be neither created nor destroyed.

20

同年八月三日半夜，慧能溘然仙逝，享年七十六岁，同年十一月，弟子才把他的遗体迎葬在曹溪山。
In the middle of the night on the third day of the eighth month, Huineng passed away at the age of seventy-six.

21

咚咚咚
bong bong bong

从此曹溪成为禅宗的圣地，慧能所提倡的顿悟南禅，慢慢地演变分成禅门五宗。
From then on, Caoxi became a holy ground for Zen Buddhism, and Huineng's Southern Sect of sudden enlightenment gradually evolved into five distinct schools.

22

马祖道一
Dayi, Patriarch Ma (Mazu)

四川成都人，俗姓马，在佛家僧侣中以俗姓为称呼的，可能只有马祖一人了。

From Chengdu in Sichuan province, his lay surname was Ma. Of all the Buddhist monks throughout history, he may be the only one to have gone by his lay surname.

马祖十二岁便出家当和尚，后来到南岳拜怀让为师。

Mazu left home to join the order at the young age of twelve. He went to Nanyu and took Huairang as his teacher.

印度第二十七祖般若多罗曾预言你的门下将产生一匹壮马，它将会踏破这个世界。

The twenty-seventh patriarch of Indian Zen, Prajñātāra, prophesied that among your disciples there would be a strong horse (ma) that would range across the land.

怀让悟道后，慧能曾告诉他说：

After Huairang's enlightenment, Huineng once said to him:

猎人的箭术
The
Hunter's
Marksmanship

石巩慧藏本来是个猎人，他最讨厌看到和尚了。
Huicang of Shigong was originally a hunter, and what he liked to see least at that time was a monk.

1

2 有一次，他追赶猎物时遇到了马祖。
One day when he was chasing down a kill, he ran into Mazu.

打猎的人。
I'm a hunter.

你是什么人？
What are you?

你会射箭吧？
Do you know how to shoot?

当然会。
Of course I can shoot.

3

4

5

6 一箭能射一个。
One animal per arrow.

你一箭能射几个？
How many can you get with one arrow?

那么你懂得射箭吗？
Then you understand shooting?

哈哈哈……
你实在不懂得射箭。
Ha, ha, ha.... you don't know the first thing about shooting.

7

210

自我的
本性
Self-
Nature

1

马祖和石头平分禅家天下，但他们之间并不敌视，反而经常共同接引学生。

In their time, Mazu and Xiquan of Shitou were the two most prominent Zen masters in all of China. Rather than seeing each other as rivals, however, they often recommended students back and forth.

药山本来是石头希迁的学生……

Yaoshan was originally a student of Shitou Xiqian...

我一直不懂"直指人心，见性成佛"之说，请师父为我指点。

I have never been able to fully understand the lines "Direct pointing at one's mind, seeing one's nature, becoming a buddha." Could you explain this for me?

肯定不对，否定也不对，肯定否定两者兼有也不对，这时，你怎么办？

It's wrong to affirm it, it's wrong to deny it, and it's wrong to both affirm and deny it. Now what?

我……
不知道。
I... I don't know.

2

3

你的因缘不在此，
还是去找马大师吧。

I don't think you are meant to be here. Why don't you go to Mazu's.

4

是。
OK.

于是药山便去参拜马祖。

So Yaoshan went to take Mazu as his teacher.

5

212

日面佛 月面佛
Buddha Of the Sun, Buddha Of the Moon

1 "日面佛"的寿命一千八百岁；
"Buddha of the Sun" lived for one thousand eight hundred years.

2 月面佛的寿命只有一昼夜。
"Buddha of the Moon" lived for only a single day and night.

3 马祖一直苦于重病，有次院主前来探病。
Once when Mazu was suffering from a long illness, the superintendent of the monastery came by to see how he was.

4 老师，贵恙如何？
How are you feeling, master?

日面佛，月面佛！
Buddha of the Sun, Buddha of the Moon!

5 可以生而生，天福也；可以死而死，天福也。懂得生之道的人，不管是活到百岁，或只活一昼夜，都是有价值的一生。
To live while one can is fortunate, and to die when one can is also fortunate. For a person who understands the principles of life, a life of a hundred years or of just one night is a life of value.

217

百丈清规
Baizhang's Regula-tions

1
马祖死后，百丈继承了马祖的法统。
After Mazu died, Baizhang inherited the orthodox dharma.

2
他制订了"百丈清规"，才奠定了僧团的组织基础，及禅宗的制度。
He then established "Baizhang's Regulations", which became the foundation for the monastic order as well as Zen Buddhism in general.

3

百丈清规对方丈及其手下人员的职责和每天的生活都有详细规定。
Baizhang's Regulations set down in detail the rules for the daily life of the abbot and all those in the monastery under him.

4
并规定一个想受戒出家的信徒，首先要立誓做到五戒：
不杀生　不偷盗　不邪淫　不妄语　不饮酒
And they required the prospective monk to vow to observe the Five Precepts:
　　Do not kill　Do not steal　Do not be licentious
　　Do not lie　Do not drink

5　接着还要做到：不坐高广大床　不歌舞娼妓
　　　　不着华鬘好香涂身　不蓄钱财珠宝　不非食
And the following:
　　Do not sleep on a high or broad bed
　　Do not observe or participate in stage shows
　　Do not adorn oneself
　　Do not acquire money or precious objects
　　Do not eat the wrong foods or at the wrong times

达到了这五戒后，才正式剃度做和尚。
Only after achieving these would he formally have his head shaven and become a monk.

7

百丈还确立制度从事耕种，不仅一般僧众，就是方丈也要工作。

Baizhang also established a system of work, in which not only the average monk worked in the fields, but the abbot as well.

8

在印度，和尚是禁止耕种的，而靠信徒的供养过活。

In India, monks were prohibited from farming and depended on offerings from the faithful.

9

百丈清规就是要革除这种乞食的寄生生活。

With his regulations, Baizhang aimed to eliminate this kind of beggarly, parasitic lifestyle.

10

为什么一个身心健全的和尚要像寄生虫一样，吸取俗人的血汗呢？

Why should a perfectly healthy monk live like some kind of parasite, sucking the life-blood out of the secular people?

11

因此他要求所有的僧众必须腾出时间来开垦荒地，从事耕种，自食其力。

So he demanded that all monks spend time opening up land to cultivation and farming their own food.

天地日月，日日作业不息；天地之间的万物也应日日作业，自强不息。

Every day, the heavens, the earth, the sun, and the moon perform their duties unceasingly. Everyday all creatures between heaven and earth should do the same, in an effort at continuous self-enrichment.

一日不作
一日不食
A Day Without
Work, A Day
Without
Food

1　百丈活到九十四高龄，还与门人一起工作。
Baizhang lived to the ripe old age of 94, all the while working side by side with the others.
门人不忍看他太劳累，就把他的工具藏起来。
Once when some monks couldn't bear to see him work so hard, they took his tools and hid them away.

嘻……
Hee, hee, hee...

唉？我的工具呢？
Hey, where are my tools?

2

3　师父吃饭啊……
Master, please eat...

不吃！
Not a bite!

一连三天百丈没有做工，但也没有吃东西。
For three days, Baizhang didn't work. But during that time, he also didn't eat.

师父！工具还给您。
Master, here are your tools back.

谢谢。
Thank you.

5　百丈因为工作了，
Because he could finally work again,

6　也就不再绝食了。
Baizhang discontinued his fast.

4

真饱！
Mmm... mm!

一日不作，一日不食。
A day without work is a day without food.

有能力工作而又有工作做，天福也。没有能力工作而又可以不必工作，天福也。
Good fortune is being able to work and having work to do. It is also not having to work when one does not have the ability to work.

7

8

炉中灵火
The Fire In the Embers

沩山灵祐是百丈的学生，也是沩仰宗的创始者。
Lingyou of Guishan was a student of Baizhang. He was also the founder of the Guishan School.

你拨拨炉子，看看还有没有火？
Please stir up the brazier and see if there's any fire left.

是。
OK.

1

2

3

师父！炉子里面已经没有火了。
Master, the fire's gone out.

4

5

我来拨拨看。
Let me try.

6

瞧！这不是火吗？
Upon hearing Baizhang's words, Guishan was suddenly enlightened.

沩山听了百丈这话，当下立刻开悟。
Look! Isn't this fire?

悟道修行，往往会迷惑得像在灰烬中找不到火一样，得与不得全在这一重要时刻，只要在绝望的临界点，再进入一层。
When cultivating enlightenment, there will always be times when confusion will make you feel like you can't find the fire in the embers. This is the time when you get it or you don't. It's just when you're on the edge of despair that you must enter a level deeper.

221

唐武宗灭佛
The
Great
Suppres-
sion

公元八四五年，佛家遭遇到一大厄运，当时的皇帝唐武宗以经济上的理由，展开了灭佛行动。
In the year 845 Buddhism in China was dealt a tragic blow when the Tang emperor Wuzong began a movement to wipe out Buddhism in China for reasons of economics.

1

3

于是破坏了四万四千六百余座寺庙，二十六万五千余僧尼被迫还俗，十五万余奴仆被政府所接收。
So more than 44,600 monasteries and temples were destroyed, more than 260,500 monks and nuns were returned to lay life, and over 15,000 servants were taken into service by the government.

有一人不耕，便有人挨饿；有一女不织，便有人受冻。可是寺庙中的僧尼不耕不织，寺庙富丽和宫殿争美，六朝因而衰败。
For every man who doesn't farm, there are others who don't have food to eat. For every woman who doesn't weave, there are others who don't have clothes to wear. Yet the monasteries' monks and nuns neither farm nor weave, and the monasteries are rich and drain resources from the palace. This is what caused the fall of the Six Dynasties.

4 这次佛门大劫中，各宗派里只有禅宗能够幸存。
Of all the various Buddhist sects suffering this disaster, only Zen survived.

5 因为禅宗不需要靠经典、佛像等，因此即使被破坏了，他们仍能发挥作用。
Because Zen didn't rely on scriptures or statues, even though everything was destroyed, the Zen mind still thrived.

6 而且禅门和尚都亲自劳作，自给自足不需要寄生于社会。
In addition, the Zen monks knew how to work and fend for themselves, not needing to depend on the rest of society for their survival.

7 这完全要归功于百丈改革禅宗制度，使禅宗在这难关中能更蓬勃地发展开来。
This success can all be attributed to the system or reformation instituted by Baizhang, which not only allowed Zen to get through the hard times, but to flourish in the end.

百丈他坚持劳作，对人类的命运有很大的意义，因为自食其力的同时，自己也掌握了自己的命运。
Baizhang's insistence on working is highly relevant to all of humanity because at the same time that you depend on your own efforts, you are also taking control of your own destiny.

香严击竹
Xiangyan
Hits
Bamboo

1
香严本是百丈门下的学生，他虽博通经典但始终未悟禅道。百丈死后，他便追随百丈的大弟子沩山。
Xiangyan was originally a student of Baizhang, and although he was well, versed in all the scriptures, he still couldn't get a handle on the meaning of Zen. After Baizhang passed away, he followed Baizhang's best disciple, Guishan.

2
你在先师百丈处听说是问一答十，问十答百，这是因为你聪明伶俐，智解辩捷。
I've heard that when you were with Baizhang, you could give ten answers for every question and a hundred answers for every ten questions. That's because you're smart and you're a good talker.

3
但生死事大，请问你在父母未生你之前，你是怎样的？
But life and death are the big questions. Tell me, before your parents were born, what were you?

4
这话问得香严茫然不知所对，便把平时看过的书翻遍，也找不到答案……
This question sent Xiangyan into a dither, and after paging through all his books, he still couldn't figure it out...

画饼究竟不能充饥啊……
I guess it's true that you can't eat a painting of a biscuit...

5
请你替我说破这个秘密吧！
Please tell me the answer!

如果我现在替你解说，将来你一定会骂我。
If I tell you now, you will be angry with me later.

6
就算我说了，我所说的还是我的，绝不会变成你的。
Even if I were to tell, it would be my answer, and it could never become yours.

224

7
这辈子我不再学佛法了，还不如做一个到处化缘乞食的和尚呢。
Why bother with all the buddha-dharma stuff? I'd be better off roaming around as a begging monk.

8
于是他到处云游，一次，他暂住在慧忠国师的遗迹古寺里……
So Xiangyan left and ended up spending some time in the temple ruins of the former National Teacher, Huizhong...

佛

他正在除草时，偶然抛一块瓦砾，击中了竹子。
Then, one day when he was out farming, his hoe came across a tile, which he picked up and tossed back into a clump of bamboo.

9

10
当！
Bonk!

清脆的一声，终使得香严顿然大悟。
On hearing the crisp hollow sound of tile against bamboo, Xiangyan suddenly attained enlightenment.

11
师父，你对我的恩惠胜过父母，如果当时你为我说破，哪有今天的顿悟呢！
Master, your kindness toward me surpasses even that of my parents. If you had told me the answer, how would I have attained enlightenment today!

当香严听到清脆竹声时，听者与声音已不再分立，而是声音与他合一，当时就是全世界！
When Xiangyan heard the crisp, hollow sound, he suddenly realized the end of the distinction between the sound and himself. He became one with the sound, and then one with the whole world!

225

226

吃饭睡觉
Eating
And
Sleeping

某次，仰山度完暑假，来看沩山……
Once after going away for summer vacation, Yangshan paid a visit to Guishan...

1

孩子，这个暑假你在那边究竟做了些什么啊？
Hey kid, what did you do over your summer vacation?

2

我耕了一块地，种下了一篮种子。
I plowed a piece of land and sowed a basket of seeds.

3

你这暑假真没白过呢！
Hey, you didn't waste your summer vacation at all!

4

白天吃饭，晚上睡觉。
During the day I ate, and at night I slept.

老师在这暑假做了些什么？
Master, how did you spend the summer vacation?

5

那么老师你这个暑假也没有白过呢！
Then you didn't waste your summer vacation, either!

轰轰烈烈与清清淡淡并无不同，只要依平常心去生活便没有白过。轰轰烈烈有轰轰烈烈的好；清淡有清淡的好。
Grandeur and simplicity aren't really so different. As long as you live according to your ordinary mind, you haven't wasted your time. Grandeur has its good side, and simplicity has its good side.

6

229

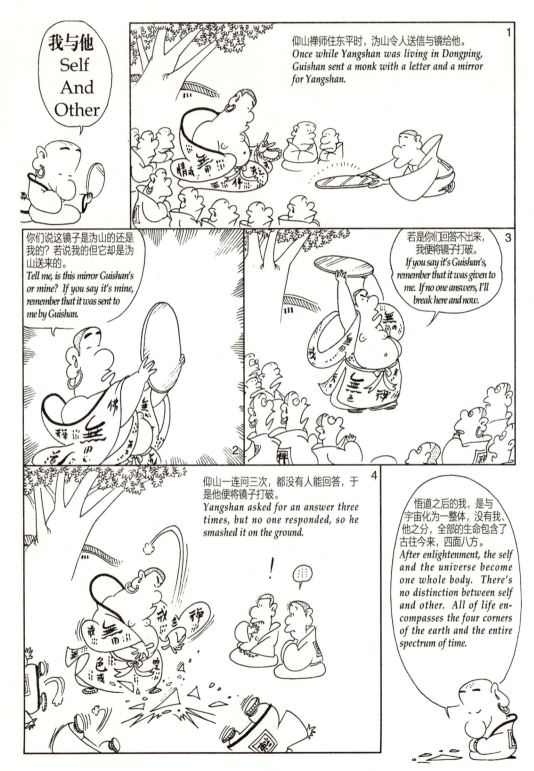

我与他
Self
And
Other

1
仰山禅师住东平时，沩山令人送信与镜给他。
Once while Yangshan was living in Dongping, Guishan sent a monk with a letter and a mirror for Yangshan.

2
你们说这镜子是沩山的还是我的？若说我的但它却是沩山送来的。
Tell me, is this mirror Guishan's or mine? If you say it's mine, remember that it was sent to me by Guishan.

3
若是你们回答不出来，我便将镜子打破。
If you say it's Guishan's, remember that it was given to me. If no one answers, I'll break here and now.

4
仰山一连问三次，都没有人能回答，于是他便将镜子打破。
Yangshan asked for an answer three times, but no one responded, so he smashed it on the ground.

悟道之后的我，是与宇宙化为一整体，没有我、他之分，全部的生命包含了古往今来，四面八方。
After enlightenment, the self and the universe become one whole body. There's no distinction between self and other. All of life encompasses the four corners of the earth and the entire spectrum of time.

230

赵州从稔
Congshen Of Zhaozhou

赵州俗姓郝，是青社缁丘人，他从小就到本州龙兴寺出家，嵩山琉璃坛受戒，后来到安徽池州拜南泉为师。
From Zi hill in Qing village, Zhaozhou's lay surname was Hao. When he was very young, he left home for the order at Longxing Monastery, and he took his vows at Song Mountain. Later, he went to Chi prefecture in Anhui province to study under Nanquan.

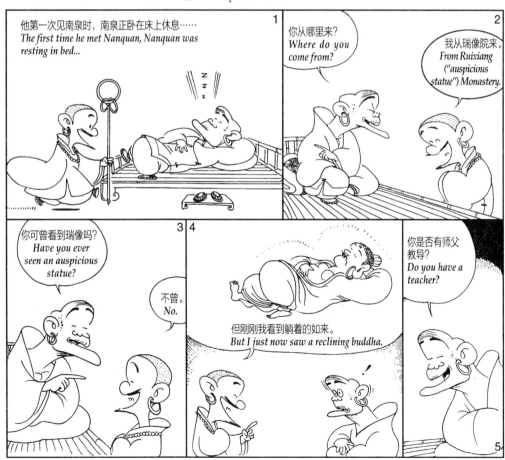

1

他第一次见南泉时，南泉正卧在床上休息……
The first time he met Nanquan, Nanquan was resting in bed...

2

你从哪里来？
Where do you come from?

我从瑞像院来。
From Ruixiang ("auspicious statue") Monastery.

3 **4**

你可曾看到瑞像吗？
Have you ever seen an auspicious statue?

不曾。
No.

但刚刚我看到躺着的如来。
But I just now saw a reclining buddha.

你是否有师父教导？
Do you have a teacher?

5

深冬，天气冷，乞望师父保重尊体。
In deep winter, the weather is cold. I hope the master takes care of himself.

哈哈哈哈!
Ha, ha, ha, ha!

师父，什么是道?
Master, what is the Dao?

6

平常心是道。
The ordinary mind is the Dao.

跟我到内室来。
Come with me.

7

8

是否有目标可循?
Is there any goal to be pursued?

当你有"目标"便有所偏差了。
As soon as you have a goal, you'll have bias as well.

如果封闭一切意念，又如何能见"道"?
How can I close off all ideas, and how can I realize the Dao?

9

10

11

"道"是不在于知和不知的，知是妄觉，不知是麻木。得道之人就能虚豁开阔，不被是非所困。
The Dao doesn't reside in realization. Realization is an illusion, and not realizing is numbness. One who has attained the Dao is empty and open, he isn't confused by right and wrong.

12

大道无门，八方开放。有千方差别的路皆可自由出入。"举一隅角即能得千隅反"了。
There is no certain way to the Dao; every way is open. There are a thousand paths that one may freely come and go by. You want to be able to extrapolate a thousand other things when only one clue is given.

南泉斩猫
Nanquan Kills a Cat

南泉禅院东西两堂的和尚在争夺一只猫……
Monks from two different halls of Nanquan Monastery were once fighting over a cat...

是我们东院的猫。
It belongs to us in the Eastern Hall.

是西院的猫。
It's the Western Hall's cat.

1

你们说句合乎佛道的话来，这只猫就得救，否则我就斩掉它。
If anyone can say one sentence in accordance with Buddhism, you'll save the cat. Otherwise, I'll kill it right here.

南泉和尚便抓起了这只猫，对大家说……
Nanquan picked up the cat and said to everyone...

2

大家都默默无语……
Everyone was silent...

3

于是，南泉便把猫斩成两截。
So Nanquan split the cat in two.

4

晚上，赵州回来后南泉把白天的事说了一遍……
That evening when Zhaozhou returned, Nanquan related the events from earlier in the day...

如果当时你在场的话，你会怎么做？
If you had been there, what would you have done?

5

赵州听完后，并不回答，只把草鞋脱下来放在头上，走了出去。
After listening, Zhaozhou didn't say anything. He just took off his shoes, put them on his head, and walked away.

假如当时你在场的话，便会救了猫儿的命。
You would have saved the cat.

南泉挥刀斩断弟子的妄念。赵州顶草鞋，本末倒置的行动为的是将杀人刀变为活人剑。
Nanquan brandished the knife and severed the delusions of his disciples. By inverting the normal order of things and putting his shoes on his head, Zhaozhou aimed to turn the deadly knife into a lifesaving sword.

6

三十年学骑马
今日被驴扑
Kicked
By a
Donkey

赵州悟道后，就到各处旅游，拜访当代的许多禅师。
After his enlightenment, Zhaozhou traveled to various parts of the land visiting many of the time's Zen masters.

1

有一次，他去拜访茱萸和尚……
Once when he paid a visit to the monk Zhuyu...

你也该定居下来弘法了。
Why don't you choose a place to abide in and disseminate the dharma.

2

我该定居在什么地方啊？
Where is my place to abide in?

3

4

哈哈! 你居然连自己的住处也不知道？
Ha ha ha! You don't even know your place to abide in?

我三十年来骑在马背上遨游，想不到今天却被驴子踢了一脚。
I've been traveling about on horseback for thirty years. Who would have thought I'd be kicked by a donkey today.

5

指出别人错误时，很可能你抱持的正是错误本身。
When pointing out other people's mistakes, the idea that you're harboring just may be the error itself.

赵州直到八十岁左右，才定居在赵州东郊的观音院……
Not until he was about eighty years old did Zhao-zhou finally settle down at Guanyin Monastery on the eastern outskirts of Zhao prefecture (Zhao-zhou)...

6

7

在他充任方丈的这段时间，他以深湛的智慧，轻松幽默地引导很多学僧走向真正的自我。
During his time as abbot, he employed a profound wisdom and relaxed sense of humor in guiding his disciples down the path toward the genuine self.

8

七岁童儿胜我者，我即请教他；百岁老翁不及我者，我即教他。
If a seven year-old child surpasses me, I learn from him. If a hundred year-old man is less than me, I teach him.

一丝不挂
Not
a Stitch
On

1
如果能做到内心里
一丝都不挂，如何？
If one can get to a point
where the mind is naked,
without a stitch on, how
would that be?

2
不挂什么？
What's not on?

3
不挂一丝。
Not a stitch is on.

4
这不是又挂了吗？
Isn't there something
on, then?

一丝不挂应连一丝不挂的
想法都要从心中扫除。"佛"
不固执于"佛"时，佛就自能显现。
唯有这样才能把握禅的真理。
Even the thought of "not a stitch on"
should be eliminated from the mind.
When "the Buddha" isn't insisted on
as "the Buddha", the Buddha suddenly appears. Only in this way can
one grasp the meaning of Zen.

237

心净
一切净
If the
Mind Is
Pure, Eve-
rything Is
Pure

道无所不在。脑的作用不见得比大
肠的回动高明多少，两者的作用是
一样重要的。
There is nowhere the Dao is not.
The brain is not necessarily that
much smarter than the gut. Both
of their functions are important.

1

2 有一女尼问赵州说：
A nun once asked
Zhaozhou:

请问什么是"密密意"？
What is the "mystical
secret"?

就是这个。
It's this.

啊！想不到你还有这个在。
Oh! I never thought you'd
still have that in you.

3

4

是你还有"这个"在。
You're the one who
has it in you.

心净一切净，心不净一
切都不净；赵州并无心，
女尼误以为有意，所以
还有"这个"在。
If the mind is pure, eve-
rything is pure. If the mind
is not pure, nothing is pure.
Zhaozhou didn't mean
anything; it was the nun
who thought he did.

5

狗的佛性
The Buddha-Nature Of a Dog

尘
Dust

1

2 清净的佛堂也会有尘埃？
Is there dust even in the purity of a Buddhist sanctuary?

清净的佛堂也会有尘埃？
Is there dust even in the purity of a Buddhist sanctuary?

3 尘埃是由外面飞进来的。
Dust drifts in from outside.

4

5 瞧！又飞进来一粒尘埃！
See, another speck just drifted in!

佛寺本是清净、了无烦恼之地，但佛寺里当然也含有尘埃。而被这种事情困惑就是迷失，就是尘埃。
A Buddhist monastery is originally a pure sanctuary, a place to be rid of distress. But of course there is also dust in it. To get caught up in this fact is confusion—just more dust.

镇州
大萝卜
Zhen
Prefec-
ture's
Big
White
Radishes

据说老师曾亲随南泉禅师，而后继其衣钵，是真的吗？
I have heard that you were once a follower of Nan-quan and that you inherited his robe and almsbowl. Is this correct?

镇州是盛产大萝卜的地方。
Zhen prefecture produces very large white radishes.

传言只是传言，若未亲眼见，仍不可信，至于相信与否，无干传言，关键在自己。若只重视风声，就容易忽略自己。
The transmission of words is just the transmission of words. If one has not experienced something for oneself, it is difficult to really believe. Belief has nothing to do with the transmission of words, but depends wholly on oneself. If you overemphasize information, it is easy to neglect the self.

241

天皇道悟
Daowu Of Tianhuang

浙江东阳人，俗姓张。二十五岁在杭州受戒，后来追随径山道钦，才接触到禅学。
From Dongyang in Zhejiang province, Daowu's lay surname was Zhang. He took his vows in Hang prefecture when he was twenty-five and then followed Daoqin of Jingshan, which was his first contact with Zen.

他随径山五年之后，又到马祖处得到印证。
After following Jingshan for five years, he went to Mazu to verify his learning.

过了两年，便去见石头希迁……
After two more years, he went to see Shitou Xiqian...

如果超脱定慧，请问还有什么法？
After one frees oneself of the concepts of meditation and knowledge, what other dharma is there to teach others?

我这里本来就没有奴隶，还谈什么超脱？
There are no slaves here. What is this talk of freeing oneself?

我还是听不懂……
I don't quite understand...

你懂得"空"吗？
Do you understand emptiness?

这一点，我早有心得。
This I've understood for a long time.

242

7

过了一段时日……
Later...

我跟随师父多时，未曾听过你为我指示心要？
I have been following you for quite a while now, but you have yet to give me any insights.

我无时无刻都在对你指示心要啊。
I am constantly giving you insights.

8

9

你指示了什么？
What insights?

你递茶来，我接了；你拿饭来，我吃；你行礼时我点头。
You bring me tea, and I take it. You bring me food, and I eat it. You bow to me, and I nod my head.

你还要我指示什么？
What more do you want?

10

11

龙潭低头想了想……
Longtan lowered his head and thought for a bit...

要能见道的话，当下就能见道。否则，一用思考便有了偏差！
If you want to behold the truth, you can do it anytime and anywhere, but thinking about it will only bring bias!

听了这话，龙潭立刻开悟。
On hearing this, Longtan immediately attained enlightenment.

12

禅的生活体验，就是能随时随地体会生活上每一细节的美好，心身永远是一体一致的，吃饭时吃饭；睡觉时睡觉！
Experiencing Zen is being able to appreciate the goodness and beauty of every detail in life. The mind and body are forever one. Eat when it's time to eat; sleep when it's time to sleep.

善慧菩萨
The Bodhisattva Shanhui

善慧即是闻名的傅大士，是一位出色的禅宗先锋。
Shanhui is also known as Mahasattva Fu, and was an outstanding precursor of early Zen Buddhism.

1
有一次梁武帝请他讲《金刚经》。
Liang Emperor Wu once invited him to give a lecture on the Diamond Sutra.

啪! Clap!

2
他上台拍了一下惊堂木，便下台了。
Shanhui ascended the platform, clapped down the square gavel, and immediately descended the platform.

?

你了解吗?
Do you understand?

完全不了解。
Not at all.

3

但我讲的经已说完了。
But I've finished my lecture.

佛、道、禅是"不可说"，因为它用语言去解释就会有偏差。因此"无法可说，是各有说法"。
Buddhahood, the Dao, and Zen are "ineffable" because anytime you have to speak about them, there will be some bias to what you say. This is why "They each speak of the dharma by saying there is no dharma to speak of."

4

246

三家同堂
Three Schools In One

有一次，善慧戴道士的帽子，穿和尚的袈裟和儒家的鞋子去见梁武帝……
Once when Shanhui went to see Emperor Wu, he wore a Daoist cap, a Buddhist robe, and Confucian-style shoes...

道帽
Daoist cap

僧衣
Buddhist robe

儒鞋
Confucian shoes

1

2
善慧指一指帽子……
Shanhui pointed to his cap...

你是和尚吗？
Are you a monk?

3
你是道士吗？
You're a Daoist priest?

4
善慧指一指鞋子……
Shanhui pointed to his shoes...

5
那么，你是方内之人了？
Then you're a Confucianist?

6
善慧又指一指衣服……
Shanhui pointed to his robe...

7
道冠儒履佛袈裟，会成三家作一家。
Daoist cap, Confucian shoes, and Buddhist robe. I've made three schools into one.

啊……
Huh...

禅是综合了儒、道、佛三家，而用之于日常生活。
Zen blends aspects of Confucianism, Daoism, and Buddhism and puts them to use in daily life.

善慧的禅诗
Shanhui's
Zen Poem

1 空手把锄头，
Holding a hoe in empty hands,

2 步行骑水牛；
Walking along, riding a bull;

3 人在桥上过，
A person crosses a bridge,

4 桥流水不流。
The bridge flows, the river stands still.

不要昧于一种形式去处理事情；不要由单一角度去看事情，变另一种形式，换另一个角度，结果往往不同。
Don't get caught up in only one way of doing things; and don't look at things from just one point of view. If you try another way, or change your point of view, the results will always be different.

洞山良价
Liangjie Of Dongshan

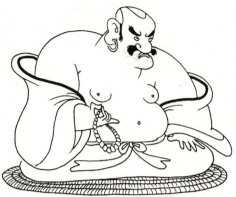

洞山是浙江会稽人，俗姓俞。幼时便出家做和尚，得道后于公元八六〇年做了江西洞山的方丈，是曹洞宗的创始人。
From Huijin in Zhejiang province, Dongshan's lay surname was Yu. He joined the order as a boy, and after his enlightenment he became the abbot at Dong Mountain (Dongshan) in Jiangxi in the year 860. He was the founder of the Caodong (Soto) sect.

于是，他开始游化各地去拜师问道。
So Dongshan began his travels to various places, learning from the great masters.

5

首先他参拜南泉，并跟随了一段时日……
He first went to see Nanquan and stayed with him for a while...

6

后来又参拜沩山。
Then he went to see Guishan.

7

无情之物真的会说法吗？如果无情会说法，为什么我却听不到？
Do insentient things really speak of the dharma? If they do, how come I can't hear it?

8

9

我父母所生的嘴巴，不是替你解说的。
With the mouth my parents gave me, I dare not tell you.

那么我应该向谁求教去？
Then who should I ask?

你去找云岩昙晟吧！
Why don't you go see Tansheng of Yunyan!

10

11

洞山便带着介绍信，去找云岩……
So with a letter of introduction, Dongshan went to see Yunyan...

251

252

法眼文益
Fayan Wenyi

浙江余杭人，俗姓鲁。幼时便出家跟随希觉律师学法。
是禅门五宗之一——法眼宗的开山祖师。
*From Yuhang in Zhejiang, Fayan's lay surname was
Lu. As a boy, he left home to join the order and studied
the dharma under the Vinaya master Xijue. He came to*

*found the Fayan School,
one of the five Zen schools.*

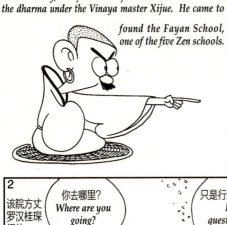

法眼游化各地，去寻求禅师的指点。
有一次路过地藏院时，正好碰到大
雨，便停下来休息。
*Fayan traveled around the land, looking
for guidance from various
teachers. Once when he
was passing by the Dicang
Monastery, a snowstorm
hit, and he stopped in to rest.*

1

2
该院方丈
罗汉桂琛
问他：
*The mo-
nas-tery's
abbot,
Luohan
Guichen,
asked
him:*

你去哪里？
*Where are you
going?*

只是行脚罢了。
*I'm on a
quest for un-
derstanding.*

3
行脚做什么呢？
Why a quest?

不知。
*I don't
know.*

4
不知最真切！
That's the best answer!

雨已经停了，我该告辞了。
*The snow has stopped.
I should be going.*

5

你曾说三界唯心，万法唯识，那么庭下那块石头是在心内，还是在心外？
You said that of the three realms there is only mind, and of the ten thousand dharmas there is only consciousness. Is that rock over there in the mind or outside the mind?

在心内。
In the mind.

6

你这位行脚僧，为何把一块大石放心中呢？
Well, Mr. Questing Monk, why would you put a huge rock inside your mind?

7

于是法眼便留下来，向罗汉讨教疑难，但罗汉每次都否定他的见解。
After this exchange, Fayan decided to stay at the monastery to study under Luohan. But every time he tried to explain something Luohan would reject it.

佛法不是这样的。
That's not how the buddha-dharma is.

8

9

我已经辞穷理屈了。
I'm out of explanations.

以佛法来说，一切都是现成的。
As far as the buddha-dharma goes, everything comes ready-made.

听了这话，法眼才恍然大悟。
On hearing this, Fayan was suddenly enlightened.

10

万物、实体本来就是现成的，并无好坏善恶的差别，但被人们变为名相后，于是孔雀美、乌鸦丑……乌鸦真的丑吗？
The myriad things and concrete substances are all ready-made, with no distinction between good or bad, but as soon as people begin to talk about them, a peacock is suddenly beautiful and a crow is ugly. Are crows really ugly?

255

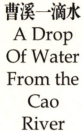

曹溪一滴水
A Drop Of Water From the Cao River

1

六祖慧能受戒后，便到曹溪建立宝林寺，并在那里住了三十六年。于是曹溪成了禅门的圣地。

After taking his vows, Huineng the sixth patriarch went to the Cao river, where he built Baolin Monastery and lived for thirty-six years. The area around the Cao River then became sacred ground.

2

什么是曹溪一滴水？
What is a drop of water from the Cao River?

你好吗？
Hello! 你好吗？
Hello!

3

曹溪一滴水。
A drop of water from the Cao River.

用言语去回答问题，就会有偏差，最完满的答案，往往就是问题本身，真理是表里如一，外面是这个话，里面就是这个内涵，内涵就是外在。

To use language in answering a question allows for bias. The most complete answer is always the question itself. The truth is the unification of exterior and interior. The exterior is these words, and the interior is this content, so the content comes to the outside.

云门文偃
Wenyan Of Yunmen

浙江嘉兴人，俗姓张。很小就出家了，学教学律都很精进，晚年移住韶州云门山的光泰禅院，举扬一家宗风。是云门宗的开山祖师。

From Jiaxing in Zhejiang province, his lay surname was Zhang. He left home to join the order when very young, and his studies in the doctrines and discipline were excellent. In his later years he moved to the Guangtai Zen Monastery on Yunmen Mountain in Guangdong, where he promoted his own style of Zen. He was the founding master of the Yunmen school.

砰砰！
knock knock!

有一次，云门去参拜睦州，要求指示。
Yunmen once paid a visit to Muzhou, looking for guidance.

1

2

你是谁？
Who is it?

我叫文偃。
My name is Wenyan.

3

你来做什么？
What are you here for?

我尚未悟见自性，来此请求指示。
I have yet to attain enlightenment, so I come for your guidance.

睦州打开门看了一眼，便把门关上了。
Muzhou opened the door, took one look, and then slammed the door shut.

接连两天，云门一再敲门，同样的被拒，直到第三天……
For two days, Yunmen knocked on the door and was rejected. Then on the third day...

4　**5**

258

参破一切只有靠自己，没有别人可以替代的。好的老师便能在最适当的时机，唤醒学生的潜能。
To see through all things, you must depend on yourself; no one else can do it for you. A good teacher can choose the most appropriate time to call out a student's potential.

睦州很快地关上门，压伤了云门的脚，刹那间，云门开悟了。
Muzhou quickly shut the door, crushing Yunmen's foot. Just at that moment, Yunmen attained enlightenment.

日日是好日
Everyday
Is a Good
Day

云门问僧徒说：
Yunmen asked his disciples:

我不问你们十五日月圆以前如何，我只问十五日以后如何？
I won't ask you how things were fifteen days ago, but rather how things will be fifteen days from now.

不知道……
I don't know...

日日是好日！
Everyday is a good day!

春有百花秋有月，夏有凉风冬有雪；
Spring has the hundred flowers, autumn has the moon, Summer has a cooling breeze, winter has the snow;

若无闲事挂心头，便是人间好时节。
As long as you keep you mind free of idle thoughts, Then, indeed, life will be a pleasant season, too.

凡事都有好的一面与坏的一面，只看到坏的，只好自哀自怨；能同时也看到好的，即能日日是好日。
All things have a good side and a bad side. If you see only the bad side, you have no choice but to complain and be sad. But if you can also see the good side, everyday will be a good day.

一字关
One Word Gate

禅宗史上，云门以"一字关"闻名，这是他唤醒学生潜能的一种策略。
Yunmen became famous in Zen history because of his "one word gate," a strategy by which he called forth his students' potential.

关！
Gate!

什么是正法眼？
What is the orthodox dharma-eye?

普！
Broad!

什么是啐啄之机？
What is a chick pecking on the inside and a hen pecking on the outside?

响。
Sound.

什么是云门宗的教义？
What is the core meaning of the Yunmen school?

亲。
Near.

杀父母向佛忏悔，杀佛祖要向谁忏悔？
If you kill your parents, you can repent to the Buddha. If you kill the Buddha, who do you repent to?

露！
Show!

什么是道？
What is the Way?

去！
Leave!

先师默然处，如何上碑？
My former master passed away. What should I write on his memorial tablet?

师。
Master.

一字关是表达不可道之道的唯一方法，都是要让学僧自己去参破。
The one word gate is the only method of saying the ineffable. Each one allows the student to see through things for himself.

言语是有限的，而真理却是无穷的。想用言语去解释真理，往往越离越远。
Language is limited, whereas the truth is inexhaustible. If you want to use language to explain the truth, the more you say, the farther away you will be.

云门三句
Yunmen's
Three
Lines

万事万物的道理是：
涵盖乾坤，截断众流，随波逐浪。
The principle of the myriad affairs and my-riad things goes like this:Encompass heaven and earth;Cut off the flow; Follow the billows and the waves.

1 真理无所不在，涵盖在整个宇宙的万物之中。
The truth is everywhere, encompassing everything in the universe.

2

3 但每一个个体都有它的独特性，也都是独一无二的。
Still, every individual body possesses its own distinctive features- is unique.

个体与这个世界是丝丝相扣，是与世俗相处，随波逐浪的。
Every individual body is inte-grally related to this world and follows the billows and waves.

4

5 绝对的真理在火中。
Absolute truth is in a flame.

262

附录·延伸阅读
APPENDIX Further reading

此部分为本书图画页的延伸阅读，各段首所示的页码与图画页对应。

P159-P160　佛陀原名悉达多，约公元前六世纪诞生于中印度憍萨罗国迦毗罗卫城，父为迦毗罗卫城主净饭王，母摩耶夫人，生七日，母逝世；二十九岁，偶出游，见衰老病死，悟世间无常，决意出家，遂放弃王位，潜马出城，至东方蓝摩国剃发为沙门；后至王舍城边阿兰若林求道，修习诸神禅定，再至伏楼频螺村之毕钵罗树（即菩提树）下，敷草结跏趺坐，终于大悟，得一切神智，成大觉世尊，为人天之大导师，时年三十五岁。

童子引至偈前礼拜，慧能曰："慧能不识字，请上人为读。"时有江州别驾，姓张名日用，便高声读，慧能闻已，遂言："亦有一偈，望别驾为书。"别驾言："汝亦作偈，其事希有。"慧能向别驾言："欲学无上菩提，不得轻于初学。下下人有上上智，上上人有没意智，若轻人，即有无量无边罪。"别驾言："汝但诵偈，吾为汝书。"慧能偈曰：

菩提本无树，明镜亦非台；

本来无一物，何处惹尘埃。

《景德传灯录》

P161-P170　第二十八祖菩提达摩者，南天竺国香至王第三子也，姓刹帝利，本名菩提多罗，后遇二十七祖般若多罗至本国受王供养，知师密迹，因试令与二兄辨所施宝珠，发明心要。既而尊者谓曰："汝于诸法已得通量，夫达摩者，通大之义也，宜名达摩，因改号菩提达摩。"师乃告尊者曰："我既得法，当往何国而作佛事？愿垂开示。"尊者曰："汝虽得法，未可远游，且止南天竺，待吾灭后六十七载，当往震旦，设大法药，直接上根，慎勿速行，衰于日下。"师又曰："彼有大士堪为法器否？千载之下有留难否？"尊者曰："汝所化之方，获菩提者不可胜数"吾灭后六十余年，彼国有难，水中文布，自善降之，汝至时，南方勿往，彼惟好有为功业，不见佛理。汝纵到彼，亦不可久留。"……

（中略）

乃至辞祖塔，次别同学。然至王所，慰而勉之。曰："当勤修白业，护持三宝，吾去非晚，一九即回。"王闻师言，涕泪交集。曰："此国何罪？彼土何祥？叔既有缘，非吾所止，惟愿不忘父母之国，事毕早回。"王即具大舟，实以众宝，躬率臣寮，送至海壖，师泛重溟，凡三周寒暑，达于南海，实梁普通八年丁未岁九月二十一日也。

广州刺史萧昂具主礼迎接，表闻武帝，帝览奏，遣使赍诏迎请。十月一日至金陵。

帝问曰："朕即位以来，造寺写经度僧不可胜纪，有何功德？"师曰："并无功德。"帝曰："何以无功德？"师曰："此但人天小果有漏之因，如影随形，虽有非实。"帝曰："如何是真功德？"答曰："净智妙圆，体自空寂，如是功德，不以世求。"帝又问如何是圣谛第一义？"师曰："廓然无圣。"帝曰："对朕者谁？"师曰："不识。"帝不领悟。师知机不契，是月十九日潜回江北。

十一月二十三日届于洛阳，当后魏孝明太和十年也。寓止于嵩山少林寺，面壁而坐终日默然，人莫之测，谓之壁观婆罗门。时有僧神光者，旷达之士也，久居伊洛，博览群书，善谈玄理，每叹曰："孔老之教，礼术风规；庄易之书，未尽妙理，近闻达摩大士住止少林，至人不遥，当造玄境。"乃往彼晨夕参承，师常端坐面墙，莫闻诲励。光自惟曰："昔人求道，敲骨取髓，刺血济饥，布发掩泥，投崖饲虎，古尚若此，我又何人？"其年十二月九日夜，天大雨雪。光坚立不动，迟明积雪过膝。师悯而问曰："汝久立雪中，当求何事？"光悲泪曰："惟愿和尚慈悲，开甘露门，广度群品。"师曰："诸佛无上妙道，旷劫精勤，难行能行，非忍而忍，岂以小德小智轻心慢心欲冀真乘，徒劳勤苦。"光闻师诲励，潜取利刀自断左臂置于师前。师知是法器，乃曰："诸佛最初求道为法忘形，汝今断臂吾前，求亦可在？"师遂因与易名曰慧可。光曰："诸佛法印，可得闻乎？"师曰："诸佛法印，匪从人得。"光曰："我心未宁，乞师与安。"师曰："将心来与汝安。"曰："觅心了不可得。"师曰："我与汝安心竟。"

后孝明帝闻师异迹，遣使赍诏征，前后三至，师不下少林，帝弥加钦尚，就赐摩衲袈裟三，领金钵银水瓶缯帛等。师牢让三返，帝意弥坚，师乃受之。自尔缁白之众，倍加信向，迄九年已，欲西返天竺，乃命门人曰："时将至矣，汝等盍各言所得乎？"时门人道副对曰："如我所见，不执文字不离文字而为道用。"师曰："汝得吾皮。"尼总持曰："我今所解，如庆喜见阿闳佛国，一见更不再见。"师曰："汝得吾肉。"道育曰："四大本空，五阴非有，而我见处无一法可得。"师曰："汝得吾骨。"最后慧可礼拜后依位而立。师曰："汝得吾髓。"乃顾慧可而告之曰："昔如来以正法眼付迦叶大士，展转嘱累而至于我，我今付汝，汝当护持，并授汝袈裟以为法信，各有所表，宜可知矣。"可曰："请师指陈。"师曰："内传法印以契证心，外付袈裟以定宗旨，后代浇薄，疑虑竞生，云吾西天之人，言汝此方之子，凭何得法，以何证之。汝今受此衣法，却后难生，但出此衣并吾法偈，用以表明，其化无碍。至吾灭后二百年，衣止不传，法周沙界，明道者多，行道者少，说理者多，通理者少，潜符密证，千万有余，汝当阐扬，勿轻未悟，一念回机，便同本得。听吾偈曰：

"吾本来兹土，传法救迷情，一花开五叶，结果自然成。"

师又曰："吾有楞伽经四卷，亦用付汝，即是如来心地要门，令诸众生开示悟入，吾自到此，凡五度中毒，我常自出而试之，置石石裂。缘吾本离南印，来此东土，见赤县神州有大乘气象，遂逾海越漠，为法求人。际会未谐，如愚若讷，今得汝传授，吾意已终。"

言已，乃与徒众往禹门千圣寺。

有一居士，年逾四十，不言名氏，聿来设礼，而问师曰："弟子身缠风恙，请和尚忏罪。"师曰："将罪来与汝忏。"居士良久云："觅罪不可得。"师曰："我与汝忏罪竟，宜依佛法僧住。"曰："今见和尚已知是僧，未审何名佛法？"师曰："是心是佛，是心是法，法佛无二，僧宝亦然。"曰："今日始知罪性不在内不在外不在中间，如其心然，佛法无二也。"大师深器之，即为剃发，云是吾宝也，宜名僧璨。其年三月十八日于光福寺受具，自兹疾渐愈，执侍经二载，大师乃告："菩提达摩远自竺乾以正法眼藏密付于吾，吾今授汝，并达摩信衣，汝当守护，无令断绝。"

第三祖僧璨大师者，不知何许人也，初以白衣谒二祖，既受度传法，隐于舒州之皖公山，属后周武帝破灭佛法。师往来太湖县司空山，居无常处，积十余载，时人无能知者。至隋开皇十二年壬子岁，有沙弥道信，年始十四，来礼师曰："愿和尚慈悲，乞与解脱法门。"师曰："谁缚汝？"曰："无人缚。"师曰："何更求解脱乎？"信于言下大悟，服劳九载。后于吉州受戒，侍奉尤谨，师屡试以玄微，知其缘熟，乃付衣法。偈曰：华种虽生地，从地种华生；若无人下种，华地尽无生。

《景德传灯录》

265

P171—172　唐韶州南华寺慧能禅师，姓卢氏，南海新兴人也。其本世居范阳，厥考讳行瑶，武德中流亭新州百姓，终于贬所，略述家系，避卢亭岛夷之不敏也。贞观十二年戊戌岁生能也。纯淑迁怀，惠性间出，虽蛮风獠俗，渍染不深，而诡行么形，驳维难测。

父既少失，母且寡居，家亦屡空，业无胈产，能负薪矣，日售荷担。偶闻鄽肆间，诵《金刚般若经》。能凝神属垣，迟迟不去。问曰："谁边受学此经？"曰："从蕲州黄梅凭茂山忍禅师，劝持此法，云即得见性成佛也。"能闻是说，若渴夫之饮寒浆也。忙归备所须，留奉亲老。

咸亭中往韶阳，遇刘志略，略有姑，无尽藏，恒读《涅槃经》，能听之，即为尼辨析中义。怪能不识文字。能曰："诸佛理论，若取文字，非佛意也。"尼深叹服，号为行者。

《高僧传》

P172—P173　于是，居人竞来瞻礼。近有宝林古寺旧地，众议营缉，俾师居之，四众雾集，俄成宝坊。

师一日忽自念曰："我求大法，岂可中道而止。"明日遂行，至昌乐县，西山石室间，遇智远禅师，师遂请益。远曰："观子神姿爽拔，殆非常人，吾闻西域菩提达摩，传心印于黄梅，汝当往彼参决。"

师辞去，直造黄梅之东禅。即唐咸亨二年也。

忍大师一见，默而识之。后传衣法，令隐于怀集四会之间。

咸亨中，有一居士，姓卢名慧能，自新州来参请，忍师问曰："汝自何来？"曰："岭南。"忍师曰："欲须何事？"曰："惟求作佛。"忍师曰："岭南人无佛性，若为得佛？"曰："人即有南北，佛性岂然。"忍师知是异人，乃诃曰："着槽厂去。"能礼足而退，便入碓坊，服劳于杵臼之间，昼夜不息。

《景德传灯录》

P174　……欲往求法，念母无依。宿昔有缘，仍蒙一客，取银十两，与慧能，令充老母衣粮，教便往黄梅，参礼五祖。慧能安置母毕，即便辞违。不经三十余日，便至黄梅，礼拜五祖。祖问："汝何方人？欲求何物？"慧能对曰："弟子是岭南新州百姓，远来礼师，惟求作佛，不求余物。"祖言："汝是岭南人，又是獦獠，若为堪作佛？"慧能曰："人虽有南北，佛性本无南北。獦獠身与和尚身不同，佛性有何差别。"五祖更欲与语，且见徒众总在左右，乃令随众作务。慧能启和尚："弟子自心，常生智慧；不离自性，即是福田，未审和尚教作何务？"祖云："獦獠根性大利，汝更勿言，着槽厂去。"慧能退至后院。有一行者，差慧能破柴踏碓，八月余日。

《六祖坛经》

P175—P177　经八月，忍师知付授时至，遂告众曰："正法难解，不可徒记吾言，持为己任，汝等各自随意述一偈，若语意冥符，则衣法皆付。"

时会下七百余僧，上座神秀者，学通内外，众所宗仰，咸共推称云："若非尊秀，畴敢当之。"神秀窃聆众誉，不复思惟，乃于廊壁书一偈。

《景德传灯录》

神秀思惟："诸人不呈心偈，缘我为教授师，我若不呈心偈，五祖何得见我心中见解深浅，我将心偈上五祖呈意，求法即善，觅祖不善，却同凡心夺其圣位。若不呈心偈，终不得法。"良见思惟，甚难，甚难。夜至三更，不令人见，遂向南廊下，中间壁上，题作呈心偈……（中略）秀上座三更于南廊下，中间壁上，秉烛题作偈，人尽不知，偈曰：

身是菩提树，心如明镜台；

时时勤拂拭，莫使惹尘埃。

神秀上座，题此偈毕，归卧房，并无人见。五祖平旦，于南廊下，忽见此偈请记……（中略）遂唤门人尽来，焚香偈前，令众人见，皆生敬心："汝等尽诵此，悟此偈者，方得见性；依此修行，即不堕落。"……（中略）

五祖遂唤秀上座于堂内，问："是汝作偈否？若是汝作，应得我法。"秀上座言："罪过，实是秀作，不敢求祖。愿和尚慈悲，看弟子有小智慧，识大意否？"五祖曰："汝作此偈，见即未到，只到门前，尚未得入。凡夫依此偈修行，即不堕落。作此见解，若觅无上菩提，即未可得，须得入门，见自本性。汝且去，一两日来，思惟，更作一偈来呈吾，若得入门，见自本性，当付汝衣法。"秀上座去数日，作不得。

《六祖坛经》

P178—P183 复两日，有一童子，于碓坊过，唱诵其偈，慧能一闻便知，此偈未见本性。虽未蒙教授，早识大意。遂问童子曰："诵者何偈？"童子曰："尔这獦獠，不知大师言，世人生死事大，欲得传付衣法，令门人作偈来看，若悟大意，即付衣法为第六祖。神秀上座，于南廊壁上，书无相偈，大师令人皆诵，依此偈修，免堕恶道；依此偈修，有大利益。"慧能曰："我此踏碓八个余月，未曾行到堂前，望上人引至偈前礼拜。"

童子引至偈前礼拜，慧能曰："慧能不识字，请上人为读。"时有江州别驾，姓张名日用，便高声读，慧能闻已，遂言："亦有一偈，望别驾为书。"别驾言："汝亦作偈，其事希有。"慧能向别驾言："欲学无上菩提，不得轻于初学。下下人有上上智，上上人有没意智，若轻人，即有无量无边罪。"别驾言："汝但诵偈，吾为汝书。"慧能偈曰：

菩提本无树，明镜亦非台；

本来无一物，何处惹尘埃。

书此偈已，徒众总惊，无不嗟讶！各相谓言："奇哉！不得以貌取人，何得多时，使他肉身菩萨。"

祖见众生惊怪，恐人损害，遂将鞋子擦了偈曰："亦未见怪。"众以为然。

次日，祖潜至碓坊，见能腰石春米，语曰："求道之人，为法忘躯，当如是乎。"乃问曰："米熟也未？"慧能曰："米熟久矣，犹欠筛在。"祖以杖击碓三下而去。慧能即会祖意，三鼓入室，祖以袈裟遮围，不令人见。为说《金刚经》，至"应无所住而生其心"，慧能言下大悟，一切万法，不离自性。遂启祖言："何期自性，本自清净；何期自性，本不生灭；何期自性，本自具足；何期自性，本无动摇；何期自性，能生万法。"

祖知悟本性，谓慧能曰："不识本心，学法无益。若识自本心，见自本性，即名丈夫、天人师、佛。"

三更受法，人尽不知，便传顿教及衣钵云："汝为第六代祖，善自护念，广度有情，流布将来，无令断绝。听吾偈曰：

有情来下种，因地果还生；

无情既无种，无性亦无生。

祖复曰："昔达摩大师初来此土，人未之信，故传此衣，以为信体，代代相承。法则以心传心，皆令自悟自解。自古佛佛惟传本体，师师密付本心，衣为争端，止汝勿传。若传此衣，命如悬丝。汝须速去，恐人害汝。"

慧能启曰："向什么处去？"

祖云："逢怀则止，遇会则藏。"……（中略）

祖相送直至九江驿，祖令上船，五祖把橹自摇。慧能言："请和尚坐，弟子合摇橹。"祖云："合是吾渡汝。"慧能云："迷时师度，悟了自度。"

《六祖坛经》

P183-P184　至仪凤元年丙子正月八日，届南海，遇印宗法师于法性寺，讲《涅槃经》。师寓止廊庑间，暮夜风飏刹幡，闻二僧对论，一云幡动，一云风动，往复酬答，未曾契理。师曰："可容俗流，辄预高论否？"直以"风幡非动，动自心耳"。印宗窃聆此语，竦然异之，翌日邀师入室，微风幡之义，师具以理告。印宗不觉起立云："行者定非常人，师为是谁？"师更无所隐，直叙得法因由。于是，印宗执弟子之礼，请受禅要。乃告四众曰："印宗具足凡夫，今遇肉身菩萨。"即指坐下卢居士云："即此是也。"因请出所传信衣，悉令瞻礼。

至正月十五日，会诸名德，为之剃发。二月八日，就法性寺智光律师，受满分戒。其戒坛即宋朝求那跋陀三藏所置也……（中略）师具戒已，于此开东山法门……（中略）

明年二月八日，师忽谓众曰："吾不愿此居，要归旧隐。"时印宗与缁白千余人，送师归宝林寺。

时韶州刺史韦据，请于大梵寺转妙法轮，并受无相心地戒。门人纪录，目为《坛经》，盛行于世。然返曹溪，两大法雨，学者不下千数。

《景德传灯录》

P185-P186　五祖弘忍门下的北宗神秀，是一杰出的人物，也是一位学解相应的禅者。但看其《北宗五方便》之说，比起向他人说禅，显得更重视经典或解释。与此相反，慧能精通《涅槃经》，也很有学问，可是其表现并不局限于传统的佛教学，这或许是基于从踏碓或卖薪所得的伟大体验。他不仅不为经典所局限，且将经典的真髓以自己的言辞直接地表现出来。

四祖道信或五祖弘忍的东山法门之禅，是注重"守心"、"看心"，然而慧能的坐禅并非看心，也非看净。所谓"看"，就是凝视某一物之意，亦即将物视为静止。他认为"佛性"就是将佛性以静止状态来看，并以实体化来凝视。相反的，慧能的禅就是"见"，而见就是"认识"。见是要以动制物，而所有能活动的本身都是要见的，并非"从动的到见的"。动作即见、看即静、见即动。所以慧能所持的目标就是动。他说："各位，我在弘忍和尚处所以听了一句话就大悟，乃由于能顿见真如本性。"

康华《中国禅》

P187-P190　六祖因明上座趁至大庾岭，祖见明至，即掷衣钵于石上云："此衣表信，可力争耶？任君将去！"明遂举之，如山不动，踟蹰悚栗曰："我来求法，非为衣也。愿行者开示！"祖云："不思善，不思恶，正与么时，哪个是明上座本来面目？"明当下大悟，遍体汗流，泣泪作礼问曰："上来密语密意外，还更有意旨否？"祖曰："我今为汝说者即非密也。汝若返照自己面目，密却在汝边。"明云："某甲虽在黄梅随众，实未省自己面目。今蒙指授入处，如人饮水，冷暖自知，今行者即是某甲师也。"祖云："汝若如是，则吾与汝同师黄梅。善自护持！"

一切经书及诸文字，小大二乘，十二部经，皆因人置，因智惠性故，故然能建立，若无世人，一切万法，本元不有。故知万法本因人兴，一切经书，因人说有。缘在人中有愚有智；愚为小人，智为大人；迷人问于智者，智人与愚人说法。令彼愚者悟解心解，迷人若悟解心开，与大智人无别。故知：不悟，即是佛是众生；一念若悟，即众生是佛。故知：一切万法，尽在自身中，何不从于自心顿现真如本性，《菩萨戒经》云："我本元自性清净。"识心见性，自成佛道。《维摩经》云："即时豁然，还得本心。"

善知识！智慧观照，内外明彻，识自本心。若识本心，即本解脱，若得解脱，即是般若三昧，即是无念。何名无念？若见一切法，心不染着，是为无念。用即遍一切处，亦不着一切处，但净本心，使六识出六门，于六尘中，无染无杂，来去自由，通用无滞，即是般若三昧，自在解脱，名无念行。

善知识！我此法门，从一般若，生八万四千智慧。何以故？为世人有八万四千尘劳，若无尘劳，智慧常现，不离自性。悟此法者，即是无念、无忆、无着，不起诳妄，用自真如性，以智慧观照，于一切法，不取不舍，即是见性成佛道。

善知识！我此法门，从上已来，顿、渐皆立无念为宗、无相无体、无住无本。何名为相？无相者，于相而离相；无念者，于念而不念；无住者，为人本性。念念不住，前念、今念、后念、念念相续，无有断绝。若一念断绝，法身即是离色身。念念时中，于一切法上无住。一念若住，念念即住，名系缚于一切上。念念不住，即无缚也，此是以无住为本。

大师往曹溪山，韶、广二州，行化四十余年，若论门人，僧之与俗，三五千人，说不尽。若论宗旨，传授《坛经》，以此为依约；若不得《坛经》，即无禀受。须知去处、年月日、姓名，递相付嘱，无《坛经》禀承，非南宗弟子也。未得禀承者，虽说顿教法，未知根本，终不免诤。但得法者，只劝修行，诤是胜负之心，与道违背。世人尽言"南能北秀"，未知根本事由。且秀禅师于南荆府当阳县玉泉寺住持修行，惠能大师于韶州城东三十五里曹溪山住。法即一宗，人有南北，因此便立南北。何以渐顿？法即一种，见有迟疾，见迟即渐，见疾即顿，法无渐顿，人有利钝，故名"渐顿"。

《六祖坛经》

P193-P196 年十五，辞亲往荆州玉泉寺，依弘景律师出家，通天二年受戒后，习毗尼藏，一日自叹曰："夫出家者，为无为法，天上人间，无有胜者。"时同学坦然禅师，知师志气高迈，劝师谒嵩山安和尚，安启发之，乃直指诣曹溪，参六祖。

祖问："什么处来？"曰："嵩山来。"祖曰："什么物，怎么来？"师无语。

遂经八载，忽然有省，乃白祖曰："某甲有个会处。"祖曰："作么生？"师曰："说似一物即不中。"祖曰："还假修证否？"师曰："修证则不无，污染即不得。"祖曰："只此不污染，诸佛之所护念。汝既如是，吾亦如是。西天般若多罗，谶汝足下，出一马驹，蹋杀天下人，并在汝心，不须速说。"师豁然契会，执侍左右一十五载。

吉州青原山行思禅师，本州安城人也，姓刘氏，幼岁出家，每群居论道，师惟默然。后闻曹溪法席，乃往参礼。问曰："当何所务即不落阶级？"祖曰："汝曾作什么来？"师曰："圣谛亦不为。"祖曰："落何阶级？"曰："圣谛尚不为，何阶级之有？"祖深器之。会下学徒虽众，师居首焉，亦犹二祖不言，少林谓之得髓矣。一日祖谓师曰："从上衣法双行，师资递授，衣以表信，法乃印心，吾今得人，何患不信，吾受衣以来，遭此多难，况乎后代。争竞必多，衣即留镇山门，汝当分化一方，无令断绝。"师既得法，住吉州青原山静居寺，六祖将示灭，有沙弥希迁问曰："和尚百年后希迁未审当依附何人？"祖曰："寻思去！"及祖顺世，迁每于静处端坐，寂若忘生。第一座问曰："汝师已逝，空坐奚为？"迁曰："我禀遗诫，故寻思尔。"第一座曰："汝有师兄行思和尚，今住吉州，汝因缘在彼，师言甚直，汝自迷耳。"迁闻语，便礼辞祖龛，直诣静居。师问曰："子何方而来？"迁曰："曹溪来。"师曰："将得什么来？"曰："未到曹溪亦不失。"师曰："怎么用去曹溪作什么？"曰："若不到曹溪，争知不失？"迁又问曰："曹溪大师还识和尚否？"师曰："汝今识吾否？"迁曰："识又争能识得？"师曰："众角虽多，一麟足矣。"

《景德传灯录》

P197 唐温州龙兴寺玄觉禅师，字明道，俗姓戴氏，永嘉人也。总角出家，龆年剃发……（中略）兄宣法师者，亦名僧也。并犹子二人，并预缁伍。觉本住龙兴寺，一门归信，连影精勤，定根确乎不移，疑树忽焉自坏。都捐我相，不污客尘。睹其寺旁，别有胜境，遂于岩下，自构禅庵……（中略）觉居其间也，丝不以衣，耕不以食……（下略）

《高僧传》

P197-P198　八岁出家，博探三藏，特通天台止观，与左溪玄朗为同门之友，住温州龙兴寺，寻自构禅庵，独居研习，常修禅观。尝以见《维摩经》而发明心地。

因看《维摩经》，发明心地。偶玄策禅师相访，与师剧谈，出言暗合诸祖。　策惊云："仁者得法师谁耶？"师曰："我听方等经论，各有师承，后于《维摩经》悟佛心宗，未有证明者。"策云："威音王以前即得，威音王以后，无师自悟，尽是天然外道。"师云："愿仁者为我证据。"策云："我言轻，曹溪有六祖大师，四方云集，并是受法者。"率师同往曹溪。

《联灯会要》

P198-P201　后因左溪玄朗禅师激励，与东阳玄策禅师，同诣曹溪。初到，振锡携瓶，绕祖三匝。祖曰："夫沙门者，具三千威仪，八万细行，大德自何方而来，生大我慢？"师曰："生死事大，无常迅速。"祖曰：何不体取无生，了无速乎？"师曰："体即无生，了本无速。"祖曰："如是如是。"于时大众，无不愕然。师方具威仪参礼，须臾告辞。祖曰："返太速乎？"师曰："本自非动，岂有速耶？"祖曰："谁知非动？"曰："仁者自生分别。"祖曰："汝甚得无生之意。"曰："无生岂有意耶？"祖曰："无意谁当分别？"曰："分别亦非意。"祖叹曰："善哉善哉，少留一宿。"时谓一宿觉。

西京光宅寺慧忠国师者，越州诸暨人也。姓冉氏，自受心印，居南阳白崖山党子谷，四十余祀，不下山门，道行闻于帝里。唐肃宗上元二年，敕中使孙朝进赍诏征赴京，待以师礼。初居千福寺西禅院，及代宗临御，复迎止光宅精蓝。十有六载随机说法，时有西天大耳三藏到京，云得他心慧眼，帝敕令与国师试验。三藏才见师，便礼拜立于右边。师问曰："汝得他心通耶？"对曰："不敢。"师曰："汝道老僧即今在什么处？"曰："和尚是一国之师，何得却去西川看竞渡？"师再问："汝道老僧即今在什么处？"曰："和尚是一国之师，何得却在天津桥上看弄猢狲？"师第三问，语亦同前。

肃宗问师得何法，师曰："陛下见空中一片云么？"帝曰："见。"师曰："钉钉着，悬挂着。"又问如何是十身调御师，乃起立，曰："还会么？"曰："不会。"师曰："与老僧过净瓶来。"又曰："如何是无诤三昧？"师曰："檀越蹋毗卢顶上行。"曰："此意如何？"师曰："莫认自己作清净法身。"又问师，师都不视之。曰："朕是大唐天子，师何以殊不顾视？"师曰："还见虚空么？"曰："见。"师曰："他还眨目视陛下否？"

《景德传灯录》

P202-P203　西京荷泽神会禅师，姓高，襄阳人也。年方幼学，厥性惇明，从师传授五经，克通幽赜；次寻庄老，灵府廓然。览《后汉书》，知浮图之说，由是于释教留神，乃无仕进之意。辞亲投本府国昌寺颢元法师下出家。其讽诵群经，易同反掌。全大律仪，匪贪讲贯。

闻岭表曹侯溪慧能禅师，盛扬法道，学者骏奔，乃效善财南方参问，裂裳裹足，以千里为跬步之间耳。

及见能，问会曰："从何所来？"答曰："无所从来。"能曰："汝不归去。"答曰："一无所归。"能曰："汝太茫茫。"答曰："身缘在路。"能曰："由自未到。"答曰："今已得到，且无滞留。"

《高僧传》

P203-P205　年十四为沙弥，谒六祖，祖曰："知识远来，大艰辛，将本来否？若有本则合识主，试说看。"师曰："以无住为本，见即是主。"祖曰："遮沙弥争合取次语？"便以杖打。师以杖下思惟曰："大善知识，历劫难逢，今既得遇，岂惜身命。"自此给侍。

他日，祖告众曰："各有一物，无头无尾，无名无字，无背无面，诸人还识否？"师乃出曰："是诸佛之本原，神会之本性。"祖曰："向汝道无名无字，汝便唤本原佛性。"师礼拜而退。

师寻往西京受戒。唐景龙中却归曹溪。祖灭后，二十年间，曹溪顿旨，沉废于荆吴，嵩岳渐门，盛行于秦洛。乃入京，天宝四年方定两宗，乃著《显宗记》，盛行于世。

一日，乡信至，报二亲亡，师入堂白槌曰："父母俱丧，请大众念摩诃般若。"众才集，师便打槌曰："劳烦大众。"

师于上元元年五月十三日中夜，奄然而化，俗寿七十五。

《景德传灯录》

P206-P208 （怀让）师乃往曹溪而依六祖，六祖问："子近离何方？"对曰："离嵩山，特来礼拜和尚。"祖曰："什么物与摩来？"对曰："说似一物即不中在。"于左右一十二载，至景云二年，礼辞祖师，祖师曰："说似一物即不中，还假修证不？"对曰："修证即不无，不敢污染。"祖曰："即这个不污染，底是诸佛之所护念。汝亦如是，吾亦如是。西天二十七祖般若多罗记汝，佛法从汝边云。向后，马驹踏杀天下人。汝勿速说此法，病在汝身也。"马和尚在一处坐，让和尚将砖去面前石上磨，马师问："作什么？"师曰："磨砖作镜。"马师曰："磨砖岂得成镜？"师曰："磨砖尚不成镜，坐禅岂得成佛也？"马师曰："如何即是？"师曰："如人驾车，车若不行，打车即是？打牛即是？"师又曰："汝为学坐禅学坐佛？为学坐佛者学坐禅？禅非坐卧；若学坐佛，佛非定相。于法无住，不可取舍，何为之乎？汝若坐佛，却是杀佛；若执坐相，非解脱理也。"马师闻师所说，从座而起礼拜问："如何用心，即合禅定无相三昧？"师曰："汝学心地法门，犹如下种。我说法要，辟彼天泽。汝缘合，故当见于道。"又问："和尚见道，当见何道？道非色，故云'何能观'？"师曰："心地法眼，能见于道，无相三昧亦复然乎？"马师曰："可有成坏不？"师曰："若契于道，无始无终，不成不坏，不聚不散，不长不短，不静不乱，不急不缓。若如是解，当名为'道'。"

《祖堂集》

P209-211 初至江西参马祖，祖问："从何处来？"曰："越州大云寺来。"祖曰："来此拟须何事？"曰："来求佛法。"祖曰："自家宝藏不顾，抛家散走作什么？我这里一物也无，求什么佛法。"师遂礼拜问曰："阿哪个是慧海自家宝藏？"祖曰："即今问我者，是汝宝藏，一切具足，更无欠少，使用自在，何假向外求觅。"师于言下自识本心，不由觉知，踊跃礼谢。师事六载。

本以戈猎为务，恶见沙门，因逐鹿群，从马祖庵前过，祖乃逆之，藏问："和尚见鹿过否？"祖曰："汝是何人？"曰："猎者。"祖曰："汝解射否？"曰："解射。"祖曰："汝一箭射几个？"曰："一箭射一个。"祖曰："汝不解射。"曰："和尚解射否？"祖曰："解射。"曰："和尚一箭射几个？"祖曰："射一群。"曰："彼此是命，何用射他一群？"祖曰："汝既知如是，何不自射？"曰："若教某甲自射，即无下手处。"祖曰："遮汉旷劫无明烦恼，今日顿息。"藏当时毁弃弓箭，自以刀截发，投祖出家。

一日，在厨中作务次，祖问："作什么？"曰："牧牛。"祖曰："作么生牧？"曰："一回入草去，便把鼻孔拽来。"祖曰："子真牧羊。"师便休。

师住后，常以弓箭接机。

《景德传灯录》

P212-P213 药山和尚嗣石头，在朗州。师讳惟俨，姓韩，绛州人也，后徙南康。年十七事潮州西山慧照禅师，大历八年受戒于衡岳寺希澡律师。师一朝言曰："大丈夫当离法自净，焉能屑屑事细行于布巾耶？"即谒石头大师密领玄言。师于贞元初，居沣阳芍药山，因号"药山和尚"焉。

师（药山）因石头垂语曰："言语动用，亦勿交涉。"师曰："无言语动用，亦勿交涉。"石头曰："这里针扎不入。"

药山在一处坐，师问："你在这里作什么？"对曰："一物也不为。"师曰："与摩则闲坐也？"对曰："若闲坐则为也。"师曰："你道不为，不为个什么？"对曰："千圣亦不识。"师以偈赞曰："从来共住不知名，任运相将作摩行；自古上贤犹不识，造次常流岂可明。"

《祖堂集》

P214 唐洪州百丈山怀海禅师，福州长乐人也。早岁离俗，三学该练，属大寂阐化南康，乃倾心依附。与西堂智藏禅师，同号入室，时二大士为角立焉。

师侍马祖行次，见一群野鸭飞过，祖曰："是什么？"师曰："野鸭子。"祖曰："什处去也？"师曰："飞过去也。"祖遂回头，将师鼻一搊，负痛失声。祖曰："又道飞过去也！"

《景德传灯录》

P215 马大师不安。

院主问："和尚，近日尊位如何？"

大师曰："日面佛、月面佛。"

《碧岩录》

P216-P217 百丈和尚凡参次，有一老人常随众听法，众人退，老人亦退，忽一日不退，师遂问："面前立者复是何人？"老人云："某甲非人也，于过去迦叶佛时，曾住此山。因学人问：'大修行底人还落因果也无？'某甲对云：'不落因果！'五百生堕野狐身。今请和尚代一转语，贵脱野狐！"遂问："大修行底人还落因果也无？"师曰："不昧因果！"

老人遂于言下大悟，作礼云："某甲已脱野狐身，住在山后，敢告和尚，乞依亡僧事例！"

师令维那白槌告众："食后送亡僧！"大众言议："一众皆安，涅槃堂又无人病，何故如是？"食后只见师领众，至山后岩下，以杖挑出一死野狐，乃依火葬。

《无门关》

P218-P219 海且曰："吾行大乘法，岂宜以诸部阿笈摩教为随行邪？"或曰："《瑜伽论》、《璎珞经》，是大乘戒律，胡不依随乎？"海曰："吾于大小乘中，博约折中，设规务归于善焉。乃创意不循律制，别立禅居。"

初自达摩传法，至六祖以来，得道眼者号长老，同西域道高腊长者，呼须菩提也，然多居律寺中，惟别院异耳。又令不论高下，尽入僧堂，堂中设长连床，施椸架，挂搭道具。卧必斜枕床唇，谓之带刀睡，为其坐禅既久，略偃亚而已。

朝参夕聚，饮食随宜，示节俭也；行普请法，示上下均力也。长老居方丈，同维那之一室也。不立佛殿，唯树法堂，表法超言象也。

其诸制度，与毗尼师，一倍相翻，天下丛林，如风偃草，禅门独行，由海之始也。

置十务，谓之寮舍，每用首领一人，管多人营事，令各司其事。或有假号窃形，混于清众，并别致喧扰之事，即堂维那，检举抽下本位挂搭，摈令出院者，贵安清众也。或彼有所犯，即以拄杖杖之，集众烧衣钵道具，遣逐从偏门而出者，示耻辱也。详此一条，制有四益：一、不污清众，生恭信故；二、不毁僧形，循佛制故；三、不扰公门，省狱讼故；四、不泄于外，护宗纲故。

《景德传灯录》

P220　百丈和尚，嗣马大师，在江西。师讳怀海，福州长乐县人也。姓黄，童年之时，随母亲入寺礼佛，指尊像问母："此是何物？"母云："此是佛。"子云："形容似人，不异于我，后亦当作焉。"自后为僧，志慕上乘，直造大寂法会，大寂一见，延之入室。师密契玄关，更无他往。师平生苦节高行，难以喻言，凡日给执劳，必先于众。主事不忍，密收作具，而请息焉，师云："吾无德，争合劳于人？"师遍求作具，既不获，而亦忘飧，故有"一日不作，一日不食"之言，流播寰宇矣。

《祖堂集》

P221　二十三，游江西，参百丈大智禅师，百丈一见，许之入室，遂居参学之首。
　　一日侍立，百丈问："谁？"师曰："灵祐。"百丈云："汝拨炉中有火否？"师拨云："无火。"百丈躬起深拨得少火，举以示之云："此不是火？"师发悟，礼谢，陈其所解。

《景德传灯录》

P222　缙素奉佛，不茹荤食肉，晚节尤谨。妻死，以道政里第为佛祠。诸节度、观察使来朝，必邀至其所，讽令出财佐营作。初，代宗喜祠祀，而未重浮屠法，每从容问所以然，缙与元载盛陈福业报应。帝意向之，繇是禁中祀佛，讽呗斋薰，号内道场，引内沙门日百余，馔供珍滋，出入乘厩马，度支具裹给。或夷狄入寇，必令众沙门诵护国仁王经为禳厌。幸其去，则横加锡予，不知纪极。胡人官至卿监封国公者，着籍禁省，势倾公王。群居赖宠，更相凌夺。凡京畿上田美产，多归浮屠。虽藏奸宿乱踵相逮，而帝终不悟。

《新唐书·王缙传》

P223　武宗即位，废浮屠法，天下毁寺四千六百，招提兰若四万，籍僧尼为民二十六万五千人，奴婢十五万人，田数千万顷，大秦穆护祆二千余人。上都、东都每街留寺二，每寺僧三十人。诸道留僧以三等，不过二十人。腴田鬻钱送户部，中下田给寺家奴婢丁壮者为两税户，人十亩。以僧尼既尽，两京悲田养病坊给寺田十顷，诸州七顷。

《新唐书·食货志》

P224—P225　祐和尚知其法器，欲激发智光，一日谓之曰："吾不问汝平生学解及经卷册子上记得者，汝未出胞胎、未辨东西时，本分事试道一句来，吾要记汝。"师懵然无对，沉吟久之，进数语，陈其所解，祐皆不许。师曰："请和尚为说。"祐曰："吾说得，是吾之见解，于汝眼目，何有益乎？"师遂归堂，遍检所集诸方语句，无一言可将酬对。乃自叹曰："画饼不可充饥。"于是尽焚之曰："此生不学佛法也，且作个长行粥饭僧，免役心神。"
　　遂泣辞沩山而去。抵南阳忠国师遗迹，遂憩止焉。一日，因山中芟除草木，以瓦砾击竹作声，俄失笑间，豁然醒悟。遽归，沐浴焚香，遥礼沩山，赞云："和尚大悲，恩逾父母，当时若为说却，何有今日事也。"

《景德传灯录》

P226　有个和尚问沩山："什么是道？"沩山回答说："无心是道。"对方说："我不会。"沩山回答说："你最好是去认识那个不会的人。"对方又问："什么是不会的人？"沩山回答说："不是别人，而是你自己啊！"

273

接着，沩山又说："你们要能当下体认这个不会的，就是你们自己的心，就是你们向往的佛。如果向外追求，得到一知半解，便以为是禅道，这真是牛头不对马嘴。正如把粪便带进来，弄污了你的心田，所以我认为这不是道。"

《禅学的黄金时代》

P227-P229 有一次，当沩山正在打坐，仰山走进他的房间，他便问："孩子，你快点说啊！不要走入阴界。"

他说这话的意思是要仰山快点开悟，而不要执着于文字和概念。仰山便回答："我连信仰都不要呢？"沩山又问："你是相信了之后不要呢，还是因为不相信才不要呢？"仰山回答说："除了我自己之外，还能信个什么啊！"沩山又说："如果是这样的话，也只是一个讲究禅定的小乘人罢了。"仰山反驳说："我连佛也不要见！"于是沩山又问："四十卷《涅槃经》中，有多少是佛说的，有多少是魔说的。"仰山回答说："都是魔说的。"听了这个答案，沩山非常高兴，便说："此后，没有人能奈何你了。"

某次，当仰山度完暑假回来看望沩山，沩山问他："孩子，我已有一个暑假没见你了，你在那边究竟做了些什么啊！"仰山回答："啊！我耕了一块地，播下了一篮种子。"沩山又说："这样看来，你这个暑假未曾闲散过去。"

仰山也问沩山这个暑假做了些什么。沩山回答："白天吃饭，晚上睡觉。"仰山便说："那么，老师，你这个暑假也未曾白度过去呢！"

引自吴经熊著 吴怡译《禅学的黄金时代》

P230-P232 沩山封一面镜寄师，师上提起云："且道是沩山镜仰山镜？有人道得，即不扑破。"众无对，师乃扑破。

唐赵州东院从稔禅师，青州临缁人也，童稚之岁，孤介弗群。越二亲之羁绊，超然离俗，乃投本州龙兴伽蓝，从师剃落，寻往嵩山琉璃坛纳戒。师勉之听习于经律，但染指而已。闻池阳愿禅师，道化翕如。

（未具戒时）便抵池阳，参南泉，值南泉偃息，而问曰："近离什么处？"师曰："近离瑞像院。"曰："还见瑞像么？"师曰："不见瑞像，只见卧如来。"曰："汝是有主沙弥无主沙弥？"师曰："有主。"曰："主在什么处？"师曰："仲冬严寒，伏惟和尚尊体万福。"南泉器之，而许入室。

异日问南泉："如何是道？"南泉曰："平常心是道。"师曰："还可趣向否？"南泉曰："拟向即乖。"师曰："不拟时如何知是道？"南泉曰："道不属知不知。知是妄觉，不知是无记。若是真达不拟之道，犹如太虚，廓然虚豁，岂可强是非耶。"

《景德传灯录》

P233 南泉和尚，因东西两堂争猫儿，乃提起云："大众，道得即救，道不得即斩却也！"众无对，泉遂斩之。晚，赵州外归，泉举似州，州乃脱履安头上而出。泉云："子若在，即救得猫儿！"

无门曰："且道赵州顶草鞋意作么生？若向者里下得一转语，便见南泉令不虚行；其或未然，险！"颂曰："赵州若在，倒行此令。夺却刀子，南泉乞命！"

《无门关》

P234-P236 师又到一老宿处。

老宿云："老大人，何不觅取住处？"师云："什么处是某甲住处？"

老宿云："老大人，住处也不识。"师云："三十年学骑马，今日被驴扑。"

僧问赵州："狗子还有佛性也无？"赵州说："无。"僧云："上至诸佛，下至蝼蚁，都有佛性，为何狗子无佛性？"赵州云："因他有前世业识。"又一次，另一僧问："狗子有无佛性？"赵州答："有。"问："既有佛性，为何投入狗胎？"赵州答："他明知故犯。"同一问题，而答语不同。第一问的答案，是用否定法，从现象作答；第二问的答案，是用肯定法，从自性作答。此即六祖问圣以凡对，问凡以圣对的方法。

问："寸丝不挂时如何？"

师云："不挂什么？"

僧云："不挂寸丝。"

师云："太好不挂。"

《祖堂集》

P237　在所有的记载中，这是赵州第一次认输，也许这位老和尚当时很饿，为了得到饼，只好输了这场比赛吧！

引自吴经熊著　吴怡译《禅学的黄金时代》

P239　赵州认为心净一切净，心不净一切都不净。譬如某天早晨，有一个尼姑要赵州告诉他什么是"密密意"，也就是说最根本的原理是什么。赵州便在她身上捏了一把。实际上他是要告诉这位尼姑最根本的原理就在她自己的身中，但这位尼姑却被赵州出其不意的动作吓得大叫说："啊！想不到你还有这个在。"赵州立刻回答说："是你还有这个在。"

僧问赵州："黄狗有佛性否？"州曰："有！"

僧曰："既有，何故撞入皮囊之中？"州曰："明知故犯也！"

又有僧问："黄狗有佛性否？"州曰："无！"

僧曰："一切众生皆具佛性，为何黄狗独无？"州曰："因之有业识在！"

事见《从容录》、《无门关》

P240　师自此道化被于北地，众请住赵州观音，上堂示众云："如明珠在掌，胡来胡现，汉来汉现，老僧把一株草为丈六金身用，把丈六金身为一株草用；佛是烦恼，烦恼是佛。"时有僧问："未审佛是谁家烦恼？"师云："与一切人烦恼。"僧云："如何免得？"师云："用免作么？"师扫地，有人问云："和尚是善知识，为什么有尘？"师曰："外来。"又僧问："清净伽蓝为什么有尘？"师曰："又一点也。"

《景德传灯录》

P241　僧问赵州和尚："尝闻你曾亲自随侍在南泉普愿禅左右，此可当真？"

州答曰："镇州产大萝卜头！"

《碧岩录》

P242—P245　荆州天皇道悟禅师，婺州东阳人也。姓张氏，神仪挺异，幼而生知，长而神俊。年十四，恳求出家，父母不听遂，誓志损减饮膳，日才一食，形体羸悴，父母不得已而许之。依明州大德披削，二十五杭州竹林寺具戒，精修梵行，推为勇猛，或风雨昏夜，宴坐丘冢，身心安静，离诸怖畏。一日游余杭，首谒径山国一禅师，受心法，服勤五载。唐大历中，抵钟陵，造马大师，重印前解，法无

275

异说。复住二夏，乃谒石头迁大师，而致问曰："离却定慧，以何法示人？"石头曰："我这里无奴婢，离个什么？"曰："如何明得？"石头曰："汝还撮得空么？"曰："恁么即不从今日去也？"石头曰："未审汝早晚从那边来？"曰："道悟不是那边人。"石头曰："我早知汝来处。"曰："师何以赃诬于人？"石头曰："汝身见在。"曰："虽如是，毕竟如何示于后人？"石头曰："汝道阿谁是后人？"师从此顿悟。

　　沣州龙潭崇信禅师，本渚宫卖饼家子也，未详姓氏，少而英异。初悟和尚为灵鉴潜请，居天皇寺，人莫之测，师家居于寺巷，常日以十饼馈之，悟受之，每食毕，常留一饼曰："吾惠汝，以荫子孙。"师一日自念曰："饼是我持去，何以返遗我耶？其别有旨乎？"遂造而问焉。悟曰："是汝持来，复汝何咎？"师闻之，颇晓玄旨，因请出家。悟曰："汝者崇福善，今信吾言，可名崇信。"由是服勤左右。

　　一日问曰："某自到来，不蒙指示心要。"悟曰："自汝到来，吾未尝不指示汝心要。"师曰："何处指示？"悟曰："汝擎茶来，吾为汝接；汝行食来，吾为汝受；汝和南时，吾便低首。何处不指示心要？"师低头良久，悟曰："见则直下便见，拟思便差。"师当下开解。

《景德传灯录》

　　P246　梁武帝请傅大士讲金刚经，大士便于座上挥案一下，便下座，武帝愕然。公问："陛下还会么？"帝云："不会！"志公云："大士讲经竟。"

《碧岩录》

　　P247–P248　有一次，善慧正在讲经，梁武帝来了，听讲的人都站起来，只有善慧仍然坐着不动。近臣们便对善慧说："君王驾临，你为什么不站起来？"善慧回答说："法地若动，一切不安。"

　　吴怡先生按：善慧的不讲经，只是表明道的不可说；他的见圣驾而不动，只是强调真人之最尊（以今语译之，就是人格尊严）；他的奇装异服，只是说明他不拘于一教，而要融三家为一体。

　　善慧穿着和尚的袈裟，道士的帽子和儒家的鞋子来朝见梁武帝，武帝看见他这身奇异的打扮便问："你是和尚吗？"善慧指一指帽子。武帝又问："你是道士吗？"善慧指一指鞋子。武帝最后说："那么，你是方内之人了？"善慧又指一指袈裟。

　　据说善慧曾有一诗："道冠儒履佛袈裟，会成三家作一家。"

　　铃木大拙说得好："禅是综合了儒、道、佛三家，而用之于我们的日常生活。"假如这种说法不错的话，那么，善慧早已开了先河。

引自吴经熊著　吴怡译《禅学的黄金时代》

　　P249–254　会有天竺僧达摩曰："我与汝毗婆尸佛所发誓，今兜率宫衣钵见在，何日当还。"因命临水观其影，见大士圆光宝盖，大士笑谓之曰："炉鞴之所多钝铁，良医之门足病人，度生为急，何思彼乐乎？"嵩指松山顶曰："此可栖矣。"大士躬耕而居之，乃说一偈曰："空手把锄头，步行骑水牛；人从桥上过，桥流水不流。"

　　筠州洞山良价禅师，会稽人也，姓俞氏。幼幼从师，因念《般若心经》，以无根尘义问其师，其师骇异曰："吾非汝师。"即指往五泄山，礼默禅师披剃。年二十一，嵩山具戒。

　　游方首谒南泉，值马祖讳辰，修斋次，南泉垂问众僧曰："来日设马师斋，未审马师还来否？"众皆无对，师乃出曰："待有伴即来。"南泉闻已赞曰："此子虽后生，甚堪雕琢。"师曰："和尚莫压良为贼。"

　　次参沩山，问曰："顷闻忠国师有无情说法，良价未究其微。"沩山曰："我这里亦有，只是难得其人。"曰："便请师道。"沩山曰："父母所生口，终不敢道。"曰："还有与师同时慕道者否？"沩山曰："此夫石室，有云岩道人，若能拨草瞻风，必为子之所重。"

　　既到云岩，问："无情说法，什么人得闻？"云岩曰："无情说法，无情得闻。"师曰："和尚闻否？"云岩曰："我若闻，汝即不得闻吾说法也。"曰："若恁么即良价不闻和尚说法也。"云岩曰："吾说法，汝尚不闻，何况无情说法也。"

　　也大奇，也大奇，无情说法不思议；若将耳听声不现，眼处闻声方可知。

　　遂辞云岩，云岩曰："什么处去？"师曰："虽离和尚，未卜所止。"曰："莫湖南去？"师曰："无。"曰："莫归乡去？"师曰："无。"曰："早晚却来？"师曰："待和尚有住处即来。"曰："自此一去难得相见。"师曰："难得不相见"。

　　又问云岩："和尚百年后，忽有人问：'还貌得师真否？'如何只对？"云岩曰："但向伊道，即这个是。"师良久，云岩曰："承当这个事，大须审细。"师犹涉疑，后因过水，睹影，大悟前旨，因有一偈曰：

　　切忌从他觅，迢迢与我疏。我今独自在，处处得逢渠。

　　渠今正是我，我今不是渠。应须恁么会，方得契如如。

　　升州清凉院文益禅师，余杭人也，姓鲁氏，七岁依新定智通院全伟禅师落发，弱龄裹具于越州开元寺，属律匠希觉师，盛化于明州鄮山育王寺，师往预听，习究其微旨，复傍探儒典，游文雅之场。觉师目为我门之游夏也。

　　师以玄机一发，杂务俱捐，振锡南迈，抵福州长庆法会，虽缘心未息而海众推之，寻更结侣，拟之湖外，既行，值天雨忽作，溪流暴涨，暂寓城西地藏院，因参琛和尚，琛问曰："上座何往？"师曰："迤逦行脚去。"曰："行脚事作么生？"师曰："不知。"曰："不知最亲切。"师豁然开悟。

《景德传灯录》

　　P255　文益参地藏院琛和尚，琛问："上座何往？"答曰："行脚去。"问："行脚事作么生？"答曰："不知。"师曰："不知最亲切。"文益豁然开悟。无知即无分别，无分别即是自性。一个成年人的赞语，不如一个小儿的骂语可爱，就是知与不知之分。聊斋考城隍有两句话："有心为善，虽善不赏；无心为恶，虽恶不罚。"可谓深得禅宗三昧之言。

引自周中一《禅话》

　　P256　法眼的宗风是"先利济"，中庸笃实。换句话说，就是用别人的话来回答别人，主要在于破斥别人说此句之执着性。此种接引方法，不像临济那样峻烈，而是以"应病与药"的手法去助人开悟，其用心良苦，由此可见其一斑。举例如下：

　　（一）慧超问法眼云："如何是佛？"法眼（清凉文益）云："汝是慧超。"于言下大悟。

　　（二）天台韶闻有僧问法眼云："如何是曹溪一滴水？"法眼云："是曹溪一滴水。"遂大悟。

《人天眼目》

　　P257—P258　法眼是一位神秘论者，不过他的神秘不是在于自然和宇宙的不可知；而是在于其生生不已。虽然他对华严经的造诣颇深，尤精于六相的原理和解释，但他却不认为现象界和实体界是同一的，因为实体是离一切相的。在他眼中实体是空的，他和学生永明道潜的这段对话中便特别说明了这点。

　　韶州云门山光奉院文偃禅师，嘉兴人也，姓张氏。幼依空王寺志澄律师出家。敏质生知，慧辩天纵，及长落发，裹具于毗陵坛，侍澄数年，探穷律部。以己事未明，往参睦州，州才见来，便闭却门，师乃扣门，州曰："谁？"师曰："某甲。"州曰："作什么？"师曰："己事未明，乞师指示。"州开门，一见，便闭却。师如是连三日扣门，至第三日，州开门，师乃掁入，州便擒住曰："道！道！"师拟议，州便推出曰："秦时𨍏轹钻。"遂掩门，损师一足。师从此悟入。

《指月录》

P259-P260　禅的体验，自有其确实性的绝对的价值，然而主体因是个性的，所以在第三者是不能知不能见，但在互相体验者之间，自有其一脉相通，这又名"惟佛与佛之境地"。但耽着在这境地时，又恐陷于魔窟里，故努力地更于差别的境界上——体验着，次之致力其平等与差别回互相入而成其圆满大智；为着这绝对智的完成，便不得不向——境上去磨炼，所谓出之以"向下门"。换言之：务须把这法乐之境给与他人共同受用者是。其表现的形式，是照各人的人格的倾向和思想的程度而有种种不同。

师云："十五日以前不问汝，十五日以后道将一句来。"自代云："日日是好日。"

《指月录》

P261　云门寻常爱说三字禅、顾鉴咦。又说一字禅。僧问："杀父杀母，佛前忏悔。杀佛杀祖，向什么处忏悔？"门云："露。"又问："如何是正法眼藏？"门云："普。"

《碧岩录》

P262-P263　云门的主要代表人物为云门文偃。他以三句（涵盖乾坤、随波逐浪、截断众流）来接引修行人。此三句据圆悟勤的说法如下："本真本空，一色一味，非无妙体，不在躊躇，洞然明白，则涵盖乾坤也。本非解会，排叠将来，不消一字，万机顿息，即截断众流也。若许他相见，从苗辨地，因语识人，即随波逐流也。"

"问：'如何是涵盖乾坤？'答曰：'包裹太虚横贯三际。'问：'如何是截断众流句？'答曰：'一念不生，万法自泯。'问：'如何是随波逐流句？'答：'随流得妙，应物全真。'"

云门宗接引学人除用三句外，也采用一字关。此种接引更能显现其宗风。举例如下：

（一）云门文偃和尚示众云："念佛法者如恒河沙，百草头上道将一句来。"良久，众无语。乃自代云："俱。"

（二）问："如何是吹毛剑？"师（云门）云："骼。"

（三）问："如何是啐啄机？"师云："响。"

《指月录》、《人天眼目》